VIKING'S LOVE
CALLED BY A VIKING
BOOK FOUR

MARIAH STONE

Stone
Publishing

GET A FREE MARIAH STONE BOOK!

Join Mariah's mailing list to be the first to know of new releases, free books, special prices, and other author giveaways.

freehistoricalromancebooks.com

ALSO BY MARIAH STONE

MARIAH'S TIME TRAVEL ROMANCE SERIES

- CALLED BY A HIGHLANDER
- CALLED BY A VIKING
- CALLED BY A PIRATE
- FATED

MARIAH'S REGENCY ROMANCE SERIES

- DUKES AND SECRETS

VIEW ALL OF MARIAH'S BOOKS IN READING ORDER

Scan the QR code for the complete list of Mariah's ebooks,
paperbacks, and audiobooks in reading order.

To M and M.
Always.

CHAPTER ONE

BUSKELAND, NORWAY, JULY 874 AD

THE MEAD HALL rang with cheers and laughter. As Kolbjorn walked towards his father's high seat, he felt lightheaded, as if he had just drunk a whole cup of ale.

But it was not alcohol that made his stomach knot with thrill.

It was hope.

The raiding season had gone well, and the mead hall swarmed with warriors eating and drinking, the buzz of stories and lousy drunken songs. The air was thick with the scent of cooked vegetables, grilled meat, and fermented honey. The day was bright outside, but semi-darkness reigned here. The light came from the fires of the oil lamps hanging on pillars carved with interwoven wolves—Jarl Bjorn's clan animal.

Kolbjorn passed by the mead tables and benches where feasting men greeted him. He nodded back as he passed. Many of them had saved his life several times during raids in the last few years. Modolfr, his best friend and sword-brother, caught Kolbjorn's arm and pulled him to the bench next to him.

"Brother," he said and gestured for a thrall to fill a drinking horn. His breath stank with mead and his cup swayed. "I want to drink to you. You won every single battle in Pictland. You saved my ass at least three times. Odin could not stop watching you, brother."

The other men nodded as they heard Modolfr. Warmth spread in Kolbjorn's stomach at the affection and approval of his closest friend. Kolbjorn chuckled and glanced in the direction of his father, Jarl Bjorn. The warmth disappeared as if blown away by a winter draft. Everyone, it seemed, approved of Kolbjorn but the only person who mattered.

Kolbjorn shook his head. "I am not a drinker. And I will eat with you after I find out what my father wanted me for."

Modolfr lowered his head. "Do you think he will finally make you his true son? If not after this raiding season, then I don't know when. Thanks to you, he has more silver than Njord has water."

Kolbjorn swallowed a knot so hard it felt like a stone. "Not quite."

Modolfr scowled at the two blond half-gods sitting by Jarl Bjorn—his sons born in wedlock with his now-deceased wife—their rich brynjas gleaming in the dim light of the fires. "Surely better than those two pig turds. All they did was show off before Jarl Bjorn."

Anger rose in Kolbjorn's blood like storm surge at the thought of Alfarr and Ebbe. How many times had he thrown Alfarr off kicking, screaming women while Ebbe did nothing? And his father? He just watched the three of them as if they were little boys who played with wooden swords. Alfarr and Ebbe threw insults at Kolbjorn when no one saw them, and he had to press down his anger, even though what he wanted

2

most was to teach them a lesson. Jarl Bjorn never defended Kolbjorn, never took his side. He allowed Alfarr and Ebbe everything, yet Kolbjorn had to follow the code of honor to the letter: courage, magnanimity, strength, loyalty, generosity, integrity, and respect.

And he still was not good enough.

One bad word about Kolbjorn and he would lose his chance at the only thing he wanted more than his next breath.

To become his father's legitimate son. To become a Bjornsson.

Then he would be the next jarl. He suspected his half-brothers had a very different take on the matter.

The serving girl—Una—brushed his arm with her breast as she poured mead into the cup. "Finally taking up drinking, Kolbjorn? Let me know if you want me to make sure you don't fly away tonight like a raven on the stormy wind."

She was pretty, with her strawberry-blonde braids around her head, her green eyes and full lips. She smelled like hay and flowers, and something sweet and feminine that made desire stir in him.

And with it, sadness. He'd had women, all right. They came to him willingly, to share his sleeping bench and give him pleasure.

But even though he had his own house, he would not marry until he could give his children an honorable name. And he still did not know what it was like to feel the real affection and care of a woman.

He smiled at Una and slid the cup to Modolfr. "Still no drinking, Una." He glanced at his father who had caught his glance and gestured for him to come closer. Needles prickled Kolbjorn's skin. Maybe this would be it.

"Save me a good piece of that boar, Una." He rose from the bench and nodded towards the spit where barbecue steamed.

"Whether I come back with good or bad news, I'll want that meat."

Kolbjorn stepped over the mead bench and walked towards his father. Jarl Bjorn was a big man, still young enough to rob many warriors of their lives in battle. He was the ideal image of a jarl: mighty and tall, a proud golden beard, combed and braided. Kolbjorn had his father's height and build, but his cur's chestnut hair and green-brown eyes must have come from his mother. He wondered if Freyr himself, the god of sunshine, blessed his father's legitimate line, although Alfarr and Ebbe's mother had assured everyone it was Odin.

The day Alfarr was born, a raven had flown into the mead hall and walked to her. And when he did, her labor started. The morning of the day when Ebbe was born, the sunrise glared as if blood was spilled across the skies.

Kolbjorn wondered what the day he was born had been like. He would never know.

He stood before his father, under his heavy gaze. And Kolbjorn was not a small man, nor was he a cowardly man. But a shiver went through him like a breeze across still waters.

"Kolbjorn, Son," his father said. "Sit."

He gestured at the chair next to him, and Kolbjorn took it. Alfarr and Ebbe whispered something to each other, throwing murderous glances at Kolbjorn. This was the first time he had sat by the honorable high seat from which his father ruled, accepted guests, negotiated, and punished. Where family sat.

Was Kolbjorn now a part of that family? The thought made him breathe faster.

"I called the three of you to discuss an important matter."

Kolbjorn leaned closer.

"You remember we visited the Danish king, Eirik, this summer? Well, there's been a development. I need his army, and I need it fast. I want the Swedes to know they can't just come knocking."

Kolbjorn frowned. This was not what he had hoped his father would say, but the fact that Father wanted to discuss political matters with him made his chest fill with hope even more.

"Did you hear rumors, Father?" Kolbjorn asked. "Do the Swedes plan an attack?"

"Shut up, bastard, this is not your business," Alfarr said into the mead horn.

Father raised his hand. "Shush, Alfarr, I need Kolbjorn's assistance."

Alfarr shook his head and gulped down the rest of his mead. Kolbjorn's heart beat in his ears. This was the first time his father had defended Kolbjorn. It sounded too good to be true.

"Now, Kolbjorn, the alliance with King Eirik also means great trading routes, and more riches than I could ever imagine. I might become a king one day. How would you like your father to be a king?"

Kolbjorn swallowed. He did not care whether his father would be a jarl or a king.

"I would like you to be a king if this is something you desire."

"I desire it. I desire it more than anything in this world. And to achieve it, I must impress Eirik. I want to create jewelry that we can sell for more silver and gold than we could ever make raiding. Southern lands will offer great prizes for it, and it's much more profitable to trade with them than to raid them. I invited the best jeweler in the North to work here, and there was never such a master as he. They say he must have apprenticed with dwarves themselves. I want you two, Alfarr and Ebbe, to deal with the Danish king alongside myself. To assure his friendship and alliance, I need to give the king the finest gift he's ever received. Eirik will come at Jul, together with many other jarls. The gift must be ready before he arrives."

Jul was the winter festival, which was in six moons. Kolbjorn clenched his jaw so hard he thought he'd break the bones. "You want Alfarr and Ebbe to assist you to woo the king. What is it that you need from me, Jarl?"

Bjorn's heavy gaze rested on Kolbjorn for a while, and if Kolbjorn was right, he saw pity flicker in his father's eyes just for a moment. Anger roared in his gut.

"I need you to lead raids during the remaining time this season and next, to bring the jeweler a hill of silver, gold, and gemstones higher than himself. I need you to do what you do best, Kolbjorn. Raid and fight."

Kolbjorn's nostrils flared. He knew where this led. If he would not be dealing with the king, that meant nothing would change for him. He had to know if he was right.

"Will you ever make me legitimate?"

The words were spilled out before the three of them like bones from a witcher's sachet, and just like the bones, destiny clung to them. Kolbjorn couldn't breathe.

"Father, you can't make him legitimate," Alfarr squealed. "This mongrel, this slave's son can't be our brother."

"'Tis not your decision." Jarl Bjorn's hand clenched in a fist. "I can do as I please."

"Father, you have more sense than that. Promising him, it's a nice little bone for a dog, but you can't be seriously thinking about making him a Bjornsson!"

The jarl pressed his lips tight and his eyebrows knit together.

"Alfarr, shut your mouth." He met Kolbjorn's eyes. "I can't have a bastard deal with the king," he said in a low voice.

The blood left Kolbjorn's face. He was such a fool. Alfarr

and Ebbe poked each other with their elbows and laughed, but Kolbjorn could not care less about their insults. Alfarr was right. Kolbjorn was just a dog whom his father lured with a bone.

"I want you to raid better," Father said. "I can't accept you in the family just yet, but if you continue to work hard and show dedication to the wolf clan, I will reconsider, Kolbjorn. I promise."

Kolbjorn gave a curt nod, and without another word he left the chair by his father and then the mead hall, walking into the freshness of the day, ignoring his friends' and sword-brothers' calls to join them.

He must have been a fool, indeed, and was an even bigger fool for realizing it and still hoping.

But in all twenty-five years of his life there had never been anything he wanted to live for besides becoming a true Bjornsson.

Even if there was the smallest chance, he'd do it. He'd turn the world upside down to get his father's approval and affection, and finally, acceptance into the family. He'd make Bjorn proud.

CHAPTER TWO

CHICAGO, SEPTEMBER 2018

RACHEL SAT on a bench on sunlit Navy Pier, watching her mother and her brother walk away. And despite the warmth of the day, the ice in her bones expanded. Her mom's arm was wrapped around James's broad shoulders for support.

Kendra had become a shadow of the vibrant, radiant artist she'd been six years ago. Her auburn hair had turned mousy, her rainbow-hued wardrobe replaced by washed out T-shirts and sweatpants, her body as thin as a match, her skin white and clammy. The only daily goal her mom had was to live till the next morning.

The doctor's appointment that morning had shaken Rachel to the core. "We found a cancerous tumor in your left kidney's renal tissue, Kendra," Dr. Khatri had said. "With end-stage renal disease, you could continue to survive on dialysis as you have for the last few years, but since cancer has come into the picture... I'm truly sorry, but my prognosis is that you have at

8

most six months to live. If you don't get a kidney transplant, that's the best we can hope for."

Rachel's body temperature must have dropped a couple of degrees. "How does she get a kidney?" she'd asked.

"Since we know that your children's kidneys are not suitable, you need to join the transplant waiting list. The surgery and medication would come to about two hundred thousand dollars. Since you don't have insurance, there's nothing we can do even if there is a donor—unless you can raise the funds required."

Rachel's fingertips found a snag in the bench's lacquered wooden panels, and a sharp stab of pain brought her back to the present moment. She pulled out the splinter and released a long, shaky breath. Lake Michigan glittered in the bright sun, blinding passersby, but Rachel stared into space. A soft breeze carried the faint scents of fresh popcorn and cinnamon pretzels.

They had come to Navy Pier after the hospital to distract themselves and think about a solution, but desperation had clung to them like a second skin. Soon, Mom had gotten too warm and James had taken her home.

Rachel had told them she needed to go to work soon, and it didn't make sense to go all the way back to the suburbs.

The truth was, waitressing was the last thing on her mind. After six years of fear, of waiting for a miracle, and of shattered hope, Rachel's personal apocalypse breathed down her neck.

The day when the person she was closest to in this world would be gone. Eleven years ago, she had lost the one person who had always made her feel safe and protected—her dad. He had not died, though. Worse.

He'd left.

Rachel remembered how her whole body had ached with the pain of loss. She'd only been eleven years old, but that was when she'd started guarding her heart. Because if anything like that happened to her again, she was afraid she might not recover.

Like if she lost her mother.

Except, this time, Rachel could stop it from happening. All she needed was $200,000. She groaned inwardly at the seeming impossibility of it.

She sure couldn't make that waitressing. And she wouldn't pin her hopes on winning the lottery.

The chatter of three old ladies—who must have sat down beside her on the bench while she was lost in thought—made Rachel glance to her right.

"Are you all right, sweetheart?" one of the ladies asked. All three stared at her, knitting frozen in their hands. The three of them looked similar, as if they were sisters. Just the color of their clothes was different: lilac, salad green and baby blue.

Rachel cleared her throat. It had been a long time since anyone had asked if she was all right. "I'm fine."

The lady sitting closest to her studied her from behind round spectacles. "You don't look fine to me, though." She had a European accent. German? "Sometimes, life gives you an answer and you just need to act. You have no idea what adventure lies ahead of you."

She and the other two exchanged meaningful smiles and began gathering their knitting into their baskets.

"Thanks," Rachel muttered, bewildered. Who said those things to a complete stranger?

Or had Rachel heard her wrong?

The lady winked at Rachel and all three walked away.

Gold glittered on the bench next to her. The sun reflected from it and hurt her eyes for a moment. Squinting, she glanced sideways at the source of the glimmer.

A golden spindle sat next to her on the bench, looking like

something straight out of a fairy tale. What was that children's story, *Sleeping Beauty* or something? Rachel turned her head a little to see better.

The spindle had very sharp edges, almost as thin as needles. It was hard to believe this was actually gold, but years spent watching her mother work in the jewelry smithy had trained her eye to know a precious metal when she saw one. The shiny surface was engraved with unending, wavy patterns, interwoven branches of trees, beasts with open jaws and sharp teeth. *Viking* came to mind.

Rachel swallowed, sweat prickled her nape, and her hand shot to the silver necklace that her mom had made when she was born. Touching the necklace always gave her comfort in times of stress. It had a unique, simple but delicate chain, and on an oval pendant, engraved in elegant handwriting, "Rachel."

Had the ladies left the spindle behind? She almost got to her feet, ready to run after them and give it back.

But something stopped her. She could take it, and no one would know. It looked like it weighed at least ten ounces. Ten ounces of gold!

Her mind raced, making calculations. Last time she checked for her mom, gold was around $1,200 per ounce. Times ten, that was $12,000!

She was not seriously thinking about stealing! She had been honest her whole life, always doing the right thing. And look where that had gotten her...

The spindle sat at a comfortable enough distance...she could just reach down and take it. Rachel glanced around and saw that there was no one close enough to notice, and she could not see the old ladies at all.

If she were to do this, there would be no way back. She'd be a thief.

But the thought of losing her mother made Rachel's breath freeze. When her father left, her whole being had hurt—every cell, every hair, every eyelash. Losing her mother would be the end of Rachel.

Rachel shifted closer to the spindle. Her heart beat as if someone tapped a wooden mallet against her chest. She was soaked through from sweat.

Her hand crawled towards the spindle. She could almost feel the cool metal despite the sun.

"God, help me," she whispered. And with a sinking stomach, she covered the spindle with her hand and yanked it under her jacket.

But as soon as she touched the metal, the world around her disappeared. Her head spun like laundry in a washing machine, her skin hurt, the hair on her whole body stood up, and something sucked her in, as if a tornado had descended just for her.

Through terror and panic, a thought came: *Is this my punishment? Am I dying?*

And then there was nothing.

CHAPTER THREE

BUSKELAND, NORWAY, SEPTEMBER 874 AD

Rachel felt cool drops hitting her face. She cracked open her eyes to the gray light of a rainy day. She lay on the ground, and around her, pines shot into the sky like spears, their green branches looming over her like a dark ceiling. The sweet smell of rotting leaves and wet earth crept into her nose.

Her body ached, her arms and legs shaking with small spasms. Warm, sunlit Navy Pier was gone, and cold seeped under her clothes and into her bones.

But it wasn't until Rachel heard something in the distance that she became fully alert, blood returning to her fingers, her heart beating faster. Animals mooing, bleating, squawking.

This could not be Chicago.

Where was she?

She sat upright, and her hand shot to her neck, searching for her necklace. Feeling the comforting shape of the locket under her fingers, she took a steadying breath. Next to her stood a big rock with a carving that looked like a long, uneven circle of a railway track with runes.

Surprisingly, Rachel understood what they said: "This rock is raised for Odin and Thor and Freyja, and the three Norns who rule people's fates. Time is the answer."

She shook her head. What in the world did that mean? Even more bewildering was the fact that she understood the words!

She looked around, and some distance down the hill, down a footworn path, stood wooden houses, long and windowless, with thatched roofs. Voices came from that direction. Beyond the village, she saw a giant snake of water that curved between the looming mountains; Viking-looking ships were docked by the shore.

Rachel's skin buzzed and panic gripped her throat till it hurt. How did she get here? The last thing she remembered was stealing the golden spindle, and then it was as if she got sucked in...where?

Was she like Dorothy in some Viking Land of Oz?

Rachel forced herself to take a deep breath, then another one.

And where was the spindle?

She looked around the grass, in the bushes and behind the rock, but it was nowhere to be found. A voice from the village rang closer than before, and Rachel froze, then darted for the woods.

She leaned against the trunk of a pine, hyperventilating, heartbeat thrashing in her ears. She felt like she had landed in a nightmare, or a weird virtual reality. She needed to find a way to return to Chicago. If she thought logically, maybe someone had picked the spindle up without seeing her nearby, and perhaps it was down in the village.

Deep breath in, deep breath out.

Rachel peeled herself off the tree and sneaked through the woods down the hill towards the houses. After a short while, she reached the first house in the village and leaned against the wall. It felt rough against her fingers and smelled like fresh lumber, tar and woodsmoke.

Rachel peeked from the corner through the branches of a bush. Further away between more houses was something like a central square, where people stopped to talk in front of stands with goods, one of them for jewelry. Rachel squinted to see if she could spot the golden spindle, but from this distance, all she could see was silver and iron.

Men wore tunics, baggy trousers, and knee-high stockings held up by laces wound around their legs. Cloaks of wool and fur were fastened over their shoulders by big silver brooches. Many had swords and axes tied to their belts, and a tingling swept up the back of Rachel's neck at the sight of the weapons. Women wore long, rectangular dresses suspended from shoulder straps and held up by silver and iron brooches.

Here, it seemed, most people were of different shades of blond, from dark honey to almost white. If she stepped onto the street, she'd stand out with her modern black jacket and jeans, her auburn hair. This all looked so strange! As if Rachel had suddenly turned up on a historical movie set.

With a sinking stomach and on shaking legs, she crept around the edge of the building, staying low. The ground, wet and muddy, clung to the soles of her shoes. Someone walked out of the house, and she darted back into the bushes.

"Guard them with your life, Kolbjorn," a low male voice said.

Rachel panted so hard, she had to put a hand over her mouth, afraid that they would hear her. Two men stood there, both giant, mountains of muscles. The one who spoke stood with his back to her, his blond hair reaching his shoulder blades. He stood with his legs wide apart, one hand on the battle ax hanging on his belt. Everything about his posture screamed power.

"I am surprised you are asking me, Father, and not your lawful sons," the younger man said. "You wanted *them* to deal with the jeweler and the king."

The sight of him made time freeze. Kolbjorn... What a strangely beautiful name.

He was taller than the older man, built in the same mighty way, his shoulders like rocks. His curly chestnut hair was cropped short, a short beard the color of chocolate covered the lower part of his face, and Rachel's fingers itched to touch it to see if it would brush soft or hard against her skin.

Hazel eyes, high cheekbones—he could be a movie star in her world, whichever world that was. Every cell in Rachel's body took him in. It was the way he held himself, his back straight, his brows knit together, his eyes squinted slightly at the man in front of him, that made her breath catch.

Something was so familiar in him, she thought that he must be a rock, a home, and a protector, and she felt like she could trust him.

Shut up. Why would I trust him?

She'd never seen him in her life, and if all went well, never would again. She did not need another person to care about.

"Deal with, yes, Son. But there is no one else who I trust more than you to keep the jewels safe. Especially *these* jewels, gold, and silver. Truthfully, you are a better warrior than your half-brothers, and I know you would rather die than let me down. Wouldn't you?"

Sweat covered Rachel's palms. Golden Viking jewels... Could the spindle be somewhere there among them?

Kolbjorn straightened his shoulders, his face lit up in determination. "I will, Father."

"Good. Now. We only have four moons till Jul, and the jeweler is working hard. We should have enough to make sure the king wants to be our ally. The Necklace of Northern Lights will make Freyja, herself, want to become the king's concubine."

The older man guffawed and slapped Kolbjorn on his shoulder. "Let's go have a dagmal. You can leave the chest. No one knows it's there, and no one would think of stealing anything from the most dangerous warrior in Norway in broad daylight."

Something sounded odd in this relationship, Rachel thought. But it was none of her business. As the two giants walked further away down the street, surprisingly a small part of her did not want to see Kolbjorn go.

When they were far away, she straightened. She had to go in to look for the spindle, and her stomach dropped at the thought. She turned around the corner and walked to the door. Probably, no one was there, but she knocked with a trembling hand to be sure she would not get any surprises. If someone answered, she would say she was looking for an old lady with snow-white hair who liked knitting.

Nothing happened, and she slowly opened the door and peered inside. It was dark, the only light coming from the dying fire on the long hearth in the center of the house. The smell of wood, hay, and dust hung heavy here—and something else, something masculine.

The walls were covered with swords, axes, shields, and leather armor. Helmets lay on the wooden chests that stood by the wall. Rachel darted to the chests, her stomach fluttering. Maybe the golden spindle would be in one of them. She raised a lid, and there were just clothes and furs. The next one had kitchen utensils. But the third one...

The contents gleamed golden in the dim light of the fire. There were necklaces, pendants, neck rings, brooches, rings, and wide bracelets that would probably fit around a big man's arm. Rachel sank her hands into the chest, the metal sharp and cool against her fingers, and took two handfuls, like a pirate.

She brought her hands closer to the light and studied the details of the jewelry. Most of the pieces had no gemstones, though a few had amber. The jewelry consisted of coils of twisted silver and gold, heads of snarling beasts, wavy, twisted branches, snake's bodies, patterns of leaves, carefully placed dots and microscopic pimples on the smooth surface. It was not even and symmetrical like modern jewelry crafted by machines. Every piece was unique, as if made for a different person.

This jewelry would go for *so* much at the antique auctions.

Well, Rachel had become a thief today. Now that she'd crossed that line it felt easier to take the next step. This was what would save her mother.

Rachel filled the pockets of her jacket. She took every last piece, though guilt curdled in her stomach. What would happen to Kolbjorn? No, she couldn't think about that. His life did not hang by a thread. Her mother needed it more.

When the chest was empty, she snuck back towards the door and peeked outside. Now that her pockets were full of stolen jewelry, she felt like she was walking on eggshells. She hadn't found the spindle, but it was too dangerous now to look for it. She had to get the hell out of here.

She'd go back to the woods and hide everything there, then try to come up with a more solid plan. It wouldn't do to be caught with her pockets full of stolen jewelry. She had a feeling Kolbjorn's dad wouldn't be too forgiving.

Luckily, the street was still empty, and she walked out, turning to take the path through the woods up the hill. Then her luck ended. Kolbjorn appeared from behind one of the houses.

Their eyes locked, just for a moment, and the sight of him knocked the breath out of her. She froze, and the world around her disappeared—there was only him and her and eternity. He seemed to have been affected, too, his lips parted, his eyes piercing her.

But she shook off the feeling. If he caught her, she'd be dead. As would her mother.

She must look strange to him in her modern clothes, but maybe if she just acted natural he'd let her pass. What would be the most normal behavior here? She swallowed and gave him a small nod. His eyes widened, but Rachel turned around and walked up the path as if she had business she needed to attend to. It took all her willpower not to dart into a jog.

Please, please, do not follow me.

No one screamed or called after her; there was no sound of quick footsteps behind her. Further and further she went. After a while, she looked back as imperceptibly as she could, and even though she was already far away, he was still standing, watching her, and the skin on her back itched.

As she walked towards the clearing, she saw the rock again and remembered the words, "Time is the answer." Could there be some clue, some key to returning, hidden around the rock? Her heart pounded, her blood vessels tingled with adrenaline.

The writing said the rock was for Odin, Thor, and Freyja. She remembered Odin and Thor from comic books and movies, they were Viking gods, right? Freyja must be one, too. Rachel's head spun, everything in her screaming that she had gone back in time and raided Vikings twice her size with sharp axes and swords, whose profession was to kill people.

She could never, ever return.

With her pulse beating in her temples, she stepped towards the rock. She gasped, feeling the pull of it, the sensation of being spun. Maybe she didn't need the spindle at all...

When she laid her hands on the rough surface, the world disappeared and so did Rachel.

CHAPTER FOUR

BUSKELAND, NORWAY, DECEMBER 874 AD

A SHARP GUST of snow hit Kolbjorn's face, and thoughts of a beautiful auburn-haired woman evaporated, leaving his heart feeling empty. She had consumed his thoughts ever since he had seen her three moons ago. He'd asked about her in the village, but there always were a lot of visitors near the end of the raiding season and nobody knew who she was. Modolfr had suggested that she might be a merchant's daughter.

Kolbjorn's dreams of her made him feel drunk, and the futile hope of seeing her again made his heart shrink in disappointment every time he thought he saw a slim figure dressed in all black.

Kolbjorn stood guard by the jeweler's workshop in the dim light of the winter morning. His eyes watered from the cold, and his nose was wet from the condensation of his breath against the bear fur of his winter cloak.

It was still calm, but a snowstorm was coming. Kolbjorn felt it like he always felt the shift of the ship deck right before meeting a good wave. The village looked empty under the dusting of snowflakes, everyone huddled in the warmth of their dwellings. He wished he was huddled by a fire with the auburn-haired beauty.

Kolbjorn had been hearing clay dishes clanking from the house behind him for a while now—the jeweler must have been making porridge and having breakfast.

Kolbjorn was probably a fool for standing here in this weather, but ever since his father had appointed him to guard the jeweler two weeks ago, Kolbjorn had only paused for a short sleep or to go to the privy. He even ate here, thanks to Una and Modolfr—they were the only ones brave enough to come near the cursed house.

A Viking was not afraid of death, but there was nothing he feared more than bad luck. Newly made jewelry had disappeared four times from the jeweler during the last few moons —and in the strangest ways...

Previous to that, of course, the jewelry had been stolen from Kolbjorn's house. He had never seen his father so furious.

"I should ban you from the village." Jarl Bjorn's eyes had thrown lightning bolts. "I should make you an outlaw. The gods have never been so ashamed than when looking at you, and neither have I."

Kolbjorn had wished for the earth to open up under his feet and swallow him. His whole body must have glowed like a red-hot coal from embarrassment. He had failed the biggest and most important task his father had ever given him. He had let his jarl down. Fury and desperation had made bile rise in his stomach.

Jarl Bjorn had forbidden him to come near the mead hall and had taken away his every possession: his silver, his house, all his weapons but one ax and one sword, and his armor.

For the last three moons, he had lived with Modolfr's

parents on their farm. He had helped them with the animals to make himself useful and thank them for letting him in, but his every move and every breath was soaked in desolation.

The only thing that had given him strength and energy was the hope of finding the auburn-haired girl. He had been torn between the burning desire to find her, just to talk to her, and the hope that his father would forgive him and invite him back to the village. He had stayed put. They could have no future. Being a bastard, he could not give her and their potential children an honorable name...if things progressed that far. And now he didn't even have a house, or a piece of silver to buy bread.

But the opportunity to redeem himself had come much sooner than he'd expected, when Modolfr had arrived to take Kolbjorn back to the village.

When Kolbjorn had stood before his father, the jarl had said, "I will forgive you and give back your status and your place on the raiding ship if you make sure no more jewelry disappears. The master will finish the king's gift, the Necklace of Northern Lights, right in time for Jul."

Hope had burned hot in Kolbjorn's chest. "I won't let you down, Jarl. Have me killed if I let anyone—or anything—touch the necklace."

But in the two weeks that Kolbjorn had guarded the house, nothing out of ordinary had happened. From the men who had guarded the jeweler before, he'd heard stories of how the jewelry had disappeared.

The first time, it had been at night. The jeweler never noticed an intruder, but in the morning the jewels were gone.

The second time, food and drinks from Valhalla had appeared on a cart by the market square: smoked sausages so aromatic they'd made men's mouths water two streets down, honeyed pies that looked like clouds, dark-brown breads that smelled like Loki's sin, drinks so sweet and bubbly they seemed as if they came from the fountain of wisdom by the roots of Yggdrasil.

The third time, a transparent woman had appeared from thin air, so beautiful it must have been the goddess Freyja herself, dancing in the air, removing her clothes, sending kisses to them. She had sent them howling like hungry wolves, and they had seen nothing else but her.

The fourth time, a giant wasp had flown in front of the guards. It looked like it was made of red iron. It had four wings that buzzed and moved like those of a dragonfly, and it had one eye. The men had chased it with axes and swords—futile of course—and while they were away, the jewelry had disappeared again.

The village witcher, who had witnessed the whole thing himself, proclaimed that the jeweler's house was damned and that the giants and the evil spirits wanted the jewelry for themselves.

But Jarl Bjorn was ready to fight anyone, even the gods, for what was his.

And Kolbjorn did not know who was stealing the jewelry, but he did not believe it was spirits. Whoever it was, he'd catch the thief and make him pay.

Through the thickening snowfall, Kolbjorn saw a slave approaching, his eyes wide. The boy stopped five feet away. "Jarl Bjorn invites the jeweler to breakfast in the mead hall. It's going to storm soon, nothing to do but wait and feast."

"Why don't you tell him yourself." Kolbjorn chuckled. He was not afraid of spirits. He was afraid to let his father down again.

The thrall made no move to do so. "I have enough bad luck in my life," he said. And with that, he turned around and jogged back to the mead hall.

Kolbjorn shook his head and went inside. But what he had thought was breakfast turned out to be mead. The heavy smell of fermented honey hung in the air. The surface of the table was covered with liquid, the clay jar stood right on the table, and Master Olfar was emptying the drinking horn.

"Kolbjorn," Olfar mumbled. "Come, son, join me in this doomed dwelling. I just finished the Necklace of Northern Lights. The spirits must be on their way. Let's meet them like Norsemen. Drunk."

Kolbjorn's jaw tightened. "The jarl is asking you to wait out the storm in the mead hall. I'll stay here and guard the necklace. Come, I see you can't get there on your own."

Even though he'd have to leave his post for a short while, Kolbjorn was confident no one would approach the haunted smithy in this weather. And what choice did he have? He couldn't exactly send the prized jeweler off on his own in his condition.

In the mead hall, the feast was starting. It seemed everyone in the village was ready to feast but Kolbjorn. Alfarr and Ebbe followed him with especially evil looks on their faces, and something else—a strange triumph that made his skin crawl.

Kolbjorn remembered the first time he had seen a similar look on a five-year-old Alfarr after his mother had whispered something to him. "Go play with the dogs, mongrel!" Alfarr had exclaimed so that the whole mead hall heard, and his mother had laughed. It had been the first stab of rejection, the first time Kolbjorn had felt dirty and excluded and low, and his cheeks had burned. His childhood wish to be part of the family, to be close to his brothers, had been crushed. And he had no illusions now that it would ever happen.

Kolbjorn delivered Master Olfar and headed back to the house. The snowfall thickened and the wind blew stronger. Kolbjorn would wait out the storm inside the jeweler's house.

He might even allow himself to sleep a bit, as it was unlikely that any thief—human or otherwise—would be able to get away with anything in this weather.

But when he opened the door, a figure slouched over the chest with the jewels.

Kolbjorn's hand shot to the ax on his belt.

The figure's head was hooded, but at the sound of his entry, the thief's head shot up, eyes wide, and recognition made thrill run through his whole body.

It was *her*.

The Necklace of Northern Lights glittered in her hand.

She was the thief!

Shock hit him like a wall of ice. Then came anger.

"You," the word escaped his mouth, and it was filled with both hope and anguish. He hated that the first woman who had made his heart race had turned out to be a common thief. "Put the necklace back."

Her fist clenched around it, and she hid it in the folds of her cloak. She straightened up and her face turned into a stern mask.

"No. Please, Kolbjorn. Let me go. I need it more than you know."

How did she know his name? He raised his ax, and her green eyes widened, but an inner hardness shone in them.

Kolbjorn made a step towards her, and she backed deeper into the house. "Give it to me," he said, "or your next breath will be the last one you take."

Her eyes flicked just for one moment to the side. She backed a few steps further, hesitation in her face, but then she yelled: "Behind you!"

Kolbjorn spun around, and his ax flew up to meet another. Alfarr's bloodthirsty face flashed in front of him. Kolbjorn threw him back with a roar.

"Treacherous worm!" he grunted.

"You are a worm. You are alone in the damned house in this storm? I'll never get a better chance to get rid of you. People will think it's the spirits." Alfarr charged him like a bull, and his head slamming into Kolbjorn's solar plexus kicked the breath out of him.

They flew across the table, his ax knocked from his hand. And as they landed on the floor, he saw a movement to his side.

The girl! The jewel! She was going to escape.

Kolbjorn gathered his strength and pressed on his half-brother's chin with one hand. With the other one, he searched for his lost ax on the ground. Clasping the handle, he hit Alfarr with the dull side of the ax, and his brother collapsed on top of Kolbjorn.

Kolbjorn pushed the unconscious man off and jumped up. She was gone.

He ran outside, and even through the thick snow he saw her dark figure running up the hill in the direction of the sacred grove.

Calling for all the gods who would listen and straining every last part of his body and soul, Kolbjorn rushed after his last chance to get back in his father's good graces.

CHAPTER FIVE

RACHEL STRUGGLED THROUGH THE SNOW, the Necklace of Northern Lights in her purse under the woolen cloak. The wind blew hard from all directions, and her lungs burned from running up the hill with snow clutching at her feet. She had to get to the rock before the giant Viking got to her.

A kidney had become available just a couple of hours ago, and Mom needed to get to the hospital within twenty-four hours or it would be too late. Rachel needed the money *now*, and the Necklace of Northern Lights was the last piece of the puzzle. When she had described the necklace to the auctioneer, he had said that he'd expect it to sell for at least a hundred thousand dollars.

Kolbjorn's tall figure climbed the hill behind her, milky through the curtain of snow. Rachel ran for her life. She'd always been a runner, and had been unstoppable on the soccer field in high school, but he was already catching up.

She could see the gray rock between the trees up the hill. Just thirty more feet.

Her muscles were on fire.

Almost there. Already reached the clearing.

Just ten more feet.

Five. Two more steps.

She could already see the rough surface, the runes. Her hands reached for the rock.

A hand grabbed her cloak and she tumbled into the snow. Her head smacked into the rock; breath whooshed out of her.

No!

Kolbjorn pinned her to the ground, and Rachel's body refused to obey her, her arms and legs like cooked spaghetti, her head spinning.

The rock was right there! Rachel wriggled, and little by little, her limbs regained strength.

"Let me go!"

Kolbjorn began rummaging under her cloak, the sensation of his hands sending electricity through her skin. "Give the necklace back."

Rachel tried to push him off her, but it was like pushing a mountain.

"Where is it?"

She felt his hand reaching for the purse, and fear shot through her.

She had to act.

She knew it was a low blow, but with the rest of her strength, she kicked him in between the legs. A moan escaped his mouth and he let her go. It was only for a second, but she managed to clamber from under him and dart for the rock.

Finally, she laid her hands on it, but nothing happened. Its icy cold, snow-damp surface burned her skin.

"What?" Rachel whispered. She was about to hit the rock with her hands again, but Kolbjorn got to his knees despite undoubtedly excruciating pain, his hands reaching for her.

Rachel had to get out of here, away from him.

With a sinking heart and anxiety spinning inside her like a whirlpool, she ran further up the hill into the woods, away from Kolbjorn.

The snowfall grew into a blizzard, its gusts kicking Rachel off her feet and stealing her breath. She turned back, and sure enough, he was after her, although slower than before.

She didn't know how long she ran. Soon, the snow was so high and the wind was so strong, that all she wanted was to lie down and take a breath. The eternity in which snowflakes stung her like bees, the need to blink, the inability to see anything through the whiteness of the world, made her slow down. She couldn't feel her body anymore, as if she floated in the air like a spirit.

No. Think about your mother!

She pushed forward, but she did not speed up.

She saw Kolbjorn's handsome face through the haze to her left, and his hazel eyes reassured her. He took her by the elbow, and she took a step and fell, but he caught her. He crouched, hugged her hips and threw her over his shoulder. The world turned upside down. Rachel wanted to protest, but she had no strength left.

"There's a cabin," Kolbjorn's voice reached her. "We will both die in this snowstorm if we stay outside."

He was right. They needed to wait it out—even if she would be trapped with him—and stay alive. Once they got to the cabin, she'd fight for the necklace with her life if she had to.

And no matter what, she would not give in to the crush she'd had on him ever since she first saw him.

INSIDE THE CABIN, the cold air still bit his face, but at least it was calm and dry. Kolbjorn closed the door, and the howling wind was muffled, but the walls shook with every gust.

The house consisted of one room. A small hearth stood in the center of the cabin on the packed-earth floor, a stash of firewood by the wall, a sleeping bench in the furthest corner, a small table, a bucket with frozen water, and a chest where kitchen utensils were usually kept.

Kolbjorn put the woman down on the sleeping bench, her eyes hazy, her forehead and the side of her face smeared with blood.

As her body touched the fur-covered wooden surface, her eyes shot wide open and she sat upright, swaying slightly. Despite the nasty wound, she looked beautiful in the dimness of the cabin, her translucent skin glowing, her auburn hair bright. She could have been Thor's daughter.

Kolbjorn cursed inwardly. She was a thief! He had spent so many days since he first saw her imagining who she was, what her life was like, what she was good at.

She was good at stealing, that's what she was.

Kolbjorn had lost his honor in front of his father because of her. And now Alfarr had tried to kill him, and who knew what lies he had told Jarl Bjorn once he woke up.

Bringing the necklace back was now a matter of life and death.

He sank to his knees in front of her. Her pupils dilated and her lips parted, a blush touching her cheeks. She smelled of wet wool, of snow, of sweet apples and fresh berries just kissed by first frost.

The scent made him itch to remove all her clothes and taste her skin.

But no. He could not have any feelings towards her other than contempt. Now that he had her, the first thing to do was get a hold of the necklace. He sank his hands into the warmth of the space between her cloak and her body, looking for where she had hidden the necklace, but his fingers only found her thin waist under her clothes...and her soft breasts.

She began pushing at his hands. "Get your hands off me, Kolbjorn!"

But he did not move. "How do you know my name?"

She began clawing at his hands like a cat. "Stop that!"

He found the leather purse, which was sewn together by a thin track of tiny metal teeth. As he pulled at a little tab, it began sliding and opening the purse like the mouth of a beast.

Who was she that she had such a magical thing?

The woman gasped and tried to jump up, but he pinned her to the bench. "You are going nowhere, thief!"

She fought with her hands. "Please, Kolbjorn, I need it. Without it my mother will die!"

Kolbjorn rummaged in the purse. "Your mother will die without a necklace? From greed, just like you?"

She snatched the purse from his hands, but he got it back and continued his search. The contents were strange. A round, long, dark-green glass vessel filled with liquid; thin, transparent bags made a material he could not identify that rustled under his fingers; and finally, the cold metal he was seeking.

He removed the object, and sure enough the Necklace of Northern Lights' diamonds glimmered in his palm.

The woman let out a pained cry and darted for it, but Kolbjorn eluded her hands and stood up.

The woman threw a pained stare at him and chewed her lower lip, her chest rising and falling. Something in Kolbjorn made him want to give her the necklace, to do anything to stop her looking at him like that. No. This was just a trap.

"Stop glowering at me." He put the necklace into the leather belt purse he always wore. "Your tricks won't work."

He then set to work starting a fire. There was always firewood in the cabin—Kolbjorn had often come here hunting with Jarl Bjorn, Alfarr, Ebbe and others, so he knew the surroundings well. The memory of rare happy moments, just a glimpse of what being part of the family would have been like, made Kolbjorn clench his fists from a dull ache. They had just been men hunting then, he and his brothers, they had not hated each other when concentrated on a common target. But wishing it could be different was futile.

When the fire cracked and the homey smell of woodsmoke filled the room, Kolbjorn stretched his hands towards the flames, the warmth burning his cold fingers. He felt the woman's unmoving eyes on him, like claws, her desperation palpable.

"Look at me all you want." He rubbed his hands. "You will not escape. Punishment always comes to those who commit crime."

The smell of crisp apples tickled his nose as she sank to the floor next to him. He felt her hands on his arm, and as he turned to her and saw her pleading eyes, something ached in him.

"You have no idea what this would do, Kolbjorn. I know you're a good man. Give the necklace back to me. You're killing someone innocent, someone who doesn't deserve to die. I'm so close to saving her, all I need is the necklace. Please!"

His throat clenched. A small part of him wished he could alleviate her pain, but he pushed that part somewhere deep and shut it up. He could not trust her.

"I am not killing anyone. It's your own fault. Did you really think that your actions wouldn't have consequences?"

She swallowed, tears glittering in her eyes, and let go of him. "The only consequence I care about is that she lives. Nothing else matters to me."

Kolbjorn was torn. Her tone, the way she spoke, told him she did not lie. He'd never known a mother's love, never known the woman who brought him into this world. He had grown up seeing how Alfarr and Ebbe's mother cared about them and loved them—and spoiled them. Kolbjorn often wondered how his life would have been if his mother were alive.

The fire warmed the air, and condensation stopped steaming out of their mouths with every breath. Wind continued to howl outside, throwing gusts of snow against the walls of the hut.

"What happened to your mother?" Kolbjorn asked, before he could stop himself.

He cursed his foolish heart. He should not care. He should not believe her. He was going to bring her to justice and, most likely, his father was going to slit her throat. The thought made his stomach turn, but that was the way of things. He could not change it. She was a thief.

"My mother is sick, and I need money to pay for her treatment. The treatment—a new kidney—is there, and I must let the doctors know by tomorrow if we will take it or not, because there are others who need it. It costs a fortune, but it's the only way to save her life. I already have about half, and all I need is this necklace. Buyers are already lined up."

"A kidney is a treatment? What kind of witchcraft is that? You are a fool if you believe any such tricks will save your mother's life."

Her nostrils flared. "That's not the point. It will work. It must!"

Kolbjorn wondered, if he had been grown enough to prevent his mother's death, even if it meant doing dishonorable things, would he have done it?

He probably would, but after that, he'd take the punishment.

And that was what she should do.

"Do you realize that when the snowstorm is over, I'll bring you to my father and he'll most likely punish you?"

The woman's face paled. "Punish me?"

"You stole the jewelry that he needs to become a king. He might even kill you."

"No. If I die, she dies! She can't die!"

Kolbjorn jumped to his feet. He'd had enough of this. "Then she dies! Sometimes mothers die."

She followed him. "All right, take the jewelry," she said, her voice choked with emotion. "Let your father be a king. I can figure something else out. Without the necklace, it's bad. But without me, she has no chance. Just let me go."

Kolbjorn made a step towards her. The blood on her forehead glistened in the light of the fire, her beautiful face illuminated by the warm, golden light, rubies playing in her hair. Despite himself, desire began burning in him. "What is your name?" he said.

"Rachel."

He frowned. The name was foreign, something he had never heard. But beautiful. Strong. Like her.

He chased the thought away. "You are going nowhere, Rachel. You will pay for what you have done."

CHAPTER SIX

RACHEL'S HEAD throbbed as if someone hacked at it with an ax. But even more painful were the desperation and anguish that burned her like salt in an open wound.

He had taken the necklace, and she could not get it back by force. And he was also going to take her to his father for some sort of punishment. The thought chilled her bones. If only he understood; if only he knew—

Maybe she could seduce him, make him see the situation differently.

That would be a dangerous game—Kolbjorn was way too attractive, and she was way too inexperienced with men, having avoided guys who showed an interest. Ever since her father had left, she'd been terrified of losing people she loved, and ever since her mom had gotten sick, she'd had no emotional capacity for anything else.

She opened her mouth, but no sound came out. It was as if she'd forgotten how to pronounce words. She frowned. Her head ached.

Kolbjorn took her hand, and warmth spread through her

body, even though they were both cold. "You are still bleeding. I'll repair the wound."

He helped her sit back next to the fire, probably so that he could see better. He rummaged in the wooden chest in the far corner of the room.

"Does anyone live here?" Rachel asked, looking around. "It looks so basic."

"No one. It's a hunting cabin on my father's lands."

He removed a cloth sachet, from which he produced what looked to Rachel like a medieval first aid kit—including what appeared to be a bone needle and a thread. Her stomach flipped at the sight.

"What the hell, Kolbjorn?"

"Stay still." He sat close to her and looked at her forehead. Rachel's skin tingled as if he touched her. "I don't know if my father will decide to kill you or not, but I am not going to have your life on my hands if he wants to pardon you and you die of a rot-wound." He pressed on her skin, making the sides of the gash come together. That hurt, but Rachel's lips parted. His touch spread warmth through her like a hot shower on a cold morning.

Kolbjorn's face was right before her. Maybe she should do something if she wanted to seduce him and get the necklace back. If she moved two inches, she'd find his lips. His eyes locked with hers, and for a second, an invisible thread connected them as it had the moment they first saw each other.

No! No way, Rachel. There can be nothing between you two.

She looked down, breaking the contact.

"It's going to hurt," he said. "When I patch up my warriors, I talk with them about hunting or fishing, or ask them to tell me their favorite story about the gods, or the women they fancy. I don't know anything about you.

Tell me about something you enjoy. That will distract you."

He punctured her skin, and pain shot through her like an electric current. She bit her lip but did not allow the whimper to leave her mouth.

"All I've cared about for the last six years has been getting my mother through her illness."

She wanted to tell him how she had dropped out of high school, how she'd looked for jobs—anything that would be legal and that would pay something: cleaning, washing dishes, waitressing—and that the biggest joy she could imagine would be having her mother healthy again. When that day came, she dreamed of going camping again, with her mom and James, just like in the happiest days with their dad. Without the dialysis machine, without the weight of dread that had been part of her since her mother first fell ill. To make a fire— like this one—to grill some s'mores, laugh and joke, and to talk —not about kidney failure, and not about bills or the hospital.

About nothing in particular and everything at the same time.

But she could not open up in front of him.

"And what did you like doing before?" Kolbjorn said, and Rachel felt the excruciating pull of the thread through her skin. She clenched her jaws to avoid crying out. "Talk," he said. "And breathe."

"I went to school," she said through clenched teeth. "I liked rock climbing and playing soccer. Why bother even talking about it? You have no idea what soccer is!"

Kolbjorn punctured her again, and Rachel sucked in a breath. Her forehead burned as if he poured hot oil on it.

"No, I don't." He frowned. "What is *soccer*?"

"It's a sport. Two teams play with a ball."

His hazel eyes flickered to hers for a moment, and tingling

went through her. "Last stitch. And where are you from then? Where people play *soccer*?"

The needle pricked her skin, probably rougher than necessary, and this time Rachel couldn't stop the yelp of pain. Dang.

"Where do you think I'm from?"

He pulled the thread further, agonizing Rachel's skin. The scar would probably stay with her her whole life. Not that it mattered.

Kolbjorn rummaged with the thread, tying it up. Even though her forehead burned with pain because of him, she did not want his hands to leave her. But they did. He put one hand on his knee, the other one pointing the needle at Rachel.

"I had thought you were a daughter of a merchant from the neighboring village. That was what folk told me when I had asked around about you. A pretty red-haired girl who dresses in black."

She forgot about the pain, about the necklace, about the wailing wind outside and that she was more than a thousand years from home. Her breath caught in her throat.

"You asked around about...me?"

He busied himself with putting the needle and the thread back in the pouch.

"I did. But it does not matter now, does it?"

He then took a dirty cloth out of the sachet and moved his hand to put it on Rachel's forehead. She jerked back.

"What the hell are you doing?"

"I want to wipe your blood. Not strangle you."

"With that dirty rag? I don't want it anywhere near my wound. Are you kidding me?"

"I always use cloth like this on my warriors."

"Kolbjorn, listen to me. What you call a rot-wound is infection; and this dirt"—she pinched the gray material between her thumb and her index finger"—is exactly what causes it.

Wash it with soap, then boil it in water for at least five minutes. Then you may apply it to open wounds. Understood?"

He watched her seriously. "Are you a witch?"

She barked out a laugh. "Something like that, to you, probably."

Kolbjorn eyed her. "Did you bewitch me, then? That moment, when I first saw you. I could not move. I wanted to follow you, but it was as if you asked me not to. Was it a spell?"

Rachel's pulse must be running faster than a Formula One race car. He was right in front of her, and she was hit with that primal scent of hay and leather and man that she'd smelled when she'd entered his house all those months ago, with his warm hazel eyes and the beard she had wanted to touch for so long...

Her hand rose as if by its own will, and her fingers traced his short beard. Crisp. But so pleasant against her fingertips. Maybe she *was* casting a spell.

Maybe he was, too.

Everything lost its meaning now, and time stood still, just as it had the first moment they saw each other. Now, all that mattered was him and her and the pull.

They came together, as inevitable as the sunrise. Her arms wrapped around his neck, her lips found his—they were firm and warm. Kolbjorn's arms wrapped around her and pulled her close, pressing her against him, every part of her skin burning where their bodies touched, even through the layers of clothing.

He licked her lower lip, and her knees melted. She let him into her mouth. Their tongues met, stroking, gliding against each other. Heat surged through her, her skin sweat-damp.

The urge to be with him, skin-to-skin, soul-to-soul, to feel him bare and true against her overtook her like intoxication, and she began untying his cloak.

His hands began fiddling with her cloak, too. Then a loud gust of wind hit the hut. The walls shook, and something cracked above their heads. A swarm of snowflakes stung Rachel's cheek, and they both jolted out of their exploration to stare at the roof, where planks hung through what was now a large hole, and thatch lay on the earth floor in a pile of snow. The wind rushed in, and the warmth of the fire—and Kolbjorn's lips and hands—the cold of the storm chilled Rachel's burning face and body.

And so, it seemed, it did his. Kolbjorn's eyes were as hard as stone, and he pulled away from her as if she threw a bucket of ice water over him.

CHAPTER SEVEN

"Thor's hairy balls," Kolbjorn spat as he left Rachel and rushed towards the hole, even though his body burned to continue what they had started.

The kiss had made all his thoughts evaporate, and with them—logic. She must be a witch. How else could she make him forget the most important goal in his life?

He must take her to Father, who would surely punish her. He could not give in to the urge to have her, to kiss her till the end of eternity, only to have her killed when the storm ended.

The wind that now wailed in brought the smell of snow and chilled Kolbjorn's skin—and his desire—returning him to sanity.

He studied the damage. The wooden beams supporting the roof were still intact. It was the thatch and two rotten planks that had broken from the pressure of snow and the strength of the storm.

"I must fix it or we'll be dead," he muttered.

"Let me help," Rachel stood next to him.

He ignored her and looked around. The shack had not been

repaired for a while, and this was the result. What Kolbjorn needed was an ax, nails—some of which must still be in the wood rot—and fresh planks, which he did not have.

But firewood lay in the far corner of the hut, and maybe he could cut the bigger pieces to cover up the hole temporarily.

He wouldn't be able to do it alone though—not before they froze to death, at any rate. He glanced at Rachel, who eyed him with a frown. "Quick"—he gestured at the planks—"find nails that are salvageable."

Rachel nodded and sank to the floor to rummage in the rotten planks lying in a small pile of snow that was growing bigger with every blast of wind. Behind the firewood stash, Kolbjorn found a log and placed it in the middle of the room. There was also a woodcutting ax. Kolbjorn took it, propped his battle ax against the wall, and began hacking at the log.

"I got six nails," Rachel said. "Is that enough?"

"No." First flitch flew from the log.

The smartest thing for Rachel to do now would be to make wooden nails with the woodcutting ax while he worked on the flitches, but there was no way Kolbjorn would trust her with an ax.

"What do you want me to do now?" she said.

"Nothing," he barked, and the next flitch flew.

"Come on, I am not some blue-blooded princess. I can do stuff. I know how to work with metal, the basics of jewelry."

"What?" The next hack sent a third flitch flying.

"My mom is a jeweler. I watched her often when she still worked."

"Jewelry won't help here."

"Well, no, not technically, but I can do *something*. Let me hammer the planks to the roof. You said we must hurry."

Kolbjorn straightened up, took a breath and regarded her. She stood straight and proud like a goddess of battle, with that wound on her forehead and blood caked against her pale skin, her lips full and dark, her cheeks red from frost, her auburn hair blowing in the wind. What he wanted most was to scoop her into his arms, take her to the sleeping bench next to him, and make her lips swell and her cheeks burn for very different reasons.

He chased the thought away.

"Can you make wooden nails?"

"I can figure it out."

Kolbjorn was surprised by her keenness. He pointed at the opposite corner of the room. "Go there. I will trust you with the ax for now. If you make one wrong move, you'll be dead sooner than you can think your next thought."

Rachel frowned. "Why are you so jumpy?"

"You could kill me to get your necklace, couldn't you? Your mother's life against mine, who would you choose? Though if you killed me, you wouldn't be able to fix the roof on your own. So you'd be dead, and with you your mother."

"But I'd never kill you, Kolbjorn." She reached out her hand. "Give me that ax. I'll figure out what to do."

Kolbjorn handed her the woodcutting ax and watched carefully as she moved away from him. Then he turned to the firewood stash and found a few wooden twigs that were thick enough and hard enough to become nails. He handed them to Rachel together with a couple of pieces of firewood.

The wind blew in more snow, and after another blast, the roof cracked. Kolbjorn's eyes shot to the direction of the hole to see if any more planks had flown off. But, for now, they remained secure.

In between the hacks of his battle ax, Kolbjorn threw glances at Rachel to make sure she was not making any moves or planning any tricks on him, but she seemed to be completely occupied by her task. The tip of her tongue peeked out the corner of her mouth, which made her look like a little girl, and Kolbjorn hid a smile.

"So, how's your dad doing?" Rachel said, and Kolbjorn froze with his ax above his head.

"Why?"

"Dunno. He is so intense."

"That's none of your business." He cut another flitch.

"I'm just curious."

He smashed the ax into the log, but it went in at the wrong angle, and a fountain of splinters sprung from under it. "Loki's hundred-year turd! You dare to ask about my father. You! Do you know what you cost me? Do you know that he took away everything?"

And he did not mean his possessions. He meant things more important. Everything he had worked so hard for his whole life. His father's approval. The chance to belong to his family.

Rachel froze, the wood and the ax in her hands. "I never meant for you to get into trouble."

The wind blew in another shower of snow, some of which hissed in the fire. "That is why I need to deliver you to him, so that he forgives me. Being a bastard does not play in my favor."

"Are you illegitimate?"

"I am his oldest—and yet, a bastard. He has two legitimate sons."

"And your mother?"

"She was a slave. She died. I never knew her."

Rachel cut another splinter. "I'm sorry that she died. That's crazy. You never knew your mother, and yet your father is in your life every day. And I am fighting to keep my mother alive when my father abandoned me like a sack of garbage."

Kolbjorn regarded her intently. What was this strange situation they were in? Rachel and he were opposite in many ways, and yet something visceral connected them and resonated deeply in him when he looked at her, when he heard her voice.

He understood well the fire in her that made her do anything to save her mother. He'd also rather die than let harm come close to his father. Somewhere in his gut, he felt that Rachel was the same.

Kolbjorn's throat clenched. The Norns who spun people's fates were so cruel. In another life, under different circumstances, he would fight for Rachel, too. Kolbjorn hit the log for the last time, and a perfect flitch flew out.

He straightened up. "That should do. Come, help me fix the roof."

They hurried to the opening, and Kolbjorn stood on a small stool to hammer the flitches with the back of his ax. Wind blew snow right into his face, choking him, but he went on. He'd gotten it right—the flitches were long enough to cover the gaps between the beams.

"I don't understand something about your dad," said Rachel when she handed him the next flitch and the nails. "He knows you are his son. He trusted you with the most important treasure—not his legitimate sons. But you are still not in the family? Why can't he just acknowledge you? Like, can he say, 'Legally, Kolbjorn is my son.' "

Kolbjorn's jaw bones clenched. She hit right in the eye, didn't she?

"Yes, he can."

"So why doesn't he? Why does your father manipulate you like that?"

Kolbjorn froze and glanced at her. "Manipulate me?" The suspicion had turned in his stomach before, but he did not want to believe it. He couldn't give up his quest after all this time. Kolbjorn drove a nail in, and the flitch covered part of the hole, which stopped the wind from blowing in his face.

"He does not manipulate me," he mumbled. "He has conditions."

"Oh. Conditions."

"Yes. And because of you, I broke them. So I'm further away from my goal than ever."

"Your goal? So you *do* want him to legally take you into the family."

It was as if she lashed his heart with a whip. Everyone in the village knew about the situation, the unspoken agreement between the jarl and his bastard hung like a tapestry on the wall of the mead hall. Modolfr was the only person who asked him about it to Kolbjorn's face, but Kolbjorn only answered yes or no or hmmed in response.

Kolbjorn had never pronounced the words, as if saying them out loud would bring a bad omen and make his goal unattainable.

But something about Rachel—her strangeness and her familiarity, the fact that her own father had abandoned her, the fact that she cared about her family as much as he did about his—made him feel that she might understand him like no one else could.

"There's nothing I want more," he croaked, "than to have my father acknowledge me."

Kolbjorn froze and so did Rachel. The words briefly hung before him in a white cloud and then evaporated on the wind.

"The worst of it is, he promised it to me a long time ago. Until I was five years old, I did not even know I was a bastard. He had even told me he was so glad when I was born, he had given me a version of his name. Kolbjorn. It means 'dark Bjorn.' The tradition is to name every first-born son after his father, but I was a bastard, so that was as close as he could get."

Kolbjorn hammered the nail deep into the wood. "Kitchen maids and slaves made sure I was fed and dressed, but every day of my life, *he* was there. I slept in the alcove in his long-house, he let me eat with him at the table. He handed me his sword the moment I was big enough to hold it and gave me my first fighting lesson."

Kolbjorn took another nail from Rachel's hands. His fingers burned when he touched her, but he did not hurry to take them away. Rachel listened and said nothing. He hammered the nail into the flitch, and it blocked a bit more of the endless storm.

"Then he got married and everything changed. Before the wedding feast, he told me he'd make me a Bjornsson if I proved myself a great warrior and an honorable man, and my whole life filled with this purpose."

Kolbjorn grimaced from the bitterness in his mouth. "Then Alfarr was born, and he couldn't name him Bjorn anymore, because I sort of took that name. But there he had his real, legal son. He forgot about me. He still talked to me from time to time, to make sure I trained well. Maybe he saw something in me."

Kolbjorn swallowed and thought that perhaps, as Rachel said, his father had just wanted to manipulate him, to keep him close in case he needed him.

He continued, "Father kept saying that because I was a bastard, he could only accept me into the family if I was worthy, if I was the example of honor and the best warrior in the whole of Norway. That if I would accomplish every single task and bring him everything he asked me to, he'd make me his real son one day. That I should make him proud."

Rachel's eyebrows knit together. "He should have done it a long time ago. I think you fulfilled his tasks and more. He should not make you work so hard for his attention. No parent should." The last words came out choked.

What Rachel said resonated in Kolbjorn as a dull ache, but

even though doubt turned in his stomach, he refused to see it her way. "You don't know anything."

"Anyone who has eyes and sees you, knows that. I bet he won't find a more worthy son than you if he searches the whole world."

Kolbjorn's eyes prickled—surely from the wind blowing right in his face, not from her words. They gave him strength and energy, though, and he continued hammering the nails into the flitches as the storm continued to fight him—and as the beautiful woman, who had made him talk better with her questions than a torturer with hot coals, stood by his side.

Every time she handed him the flitches, he touched her fingers, lingering. And she accepted his touch with a smile, the moments of connection stretching into eternity. As warmth spread through him at the contact, it warred with the cold certainty that their future would be all too brief.

CHAPTER EIGHT

RACHEL WATCHED Kolbjorn feed the fire with a log, and it crackled as flames licked at the fresh wood. Darkness had returned to the room after they'd finally repaired the roof—just in time for the short winter day to end and a howling night to engulf the world.

Rachel and Kolbjorn sat by the fire, their legs almost touching. The proximity of Kolbjorn's powerful body made her tingle all over, on top of the buzzing of her muscles from the physical strain of the day. The comforting smell of woodsmoke had returned in the room, but despite the fire, it was still cold in the shack, the patchwork that Kolbjorn and she had done with the roof had only provided a temporary solution.

Rachel eyed his gorgeous profile as he stared into the fire, his hazel eyes and chestnut-brown hair—such a lovely color—his high cheekbones and straight nose.

Rachel had a strange feeling, as if she and Kolbjorn were in between worlds, both shielded and threatened by the storm that cut them off from everything else, including their worries.

And at least for now, just for this moment, when she could do nothing but wait, Rachel allowed herself to relax.

"Are you hungry?" she asked. When he glanced up at her, she smiled, the feeling foreign on her lips.

"Starving, but there's nothing in the hut."

"There is." She rummaged in her purse.

She removed the bottle of wine, two packs with hot dogs and a bag of buns, all of which she had planned to use to distract the guards if necessary. But neither that nor her main distraction, a plastic bag filled with three hundred synthetic sapphires—she had planned to throw them on the streets and let people fight for them—was needed in the end.

She handed the hot dogs to Kolbjorn. He eyed them with curiosity and rustled the plastic wrapping between his fingers.

"What is this material? Is it leather? Slime? How is it made?"

Rachel opened her mouth to tell him the truth but stopped herself. She was not sure if she should trust him. It would give him even more power over her than he had now. The thought made her feel guilty because Kolbjorn had trusted her today.

"I don't know how the material is made." She had no idea how plastic was actually produced. "But we'll eat what's inside —the sausages and the bread—and we'll drink the wine. We have fire, we have hot dogs—that's what the sausages are called—and we have sticks. We'll eat the best dinner in ages. For me, anyways. Can you roast them? I'll open the wine."

While Rachel twisted the metal cap off the Australian Shiraz, Kolbjorn broke open the pack of hot dogs and eyed them with curiosity.

"Never seen sausages like that," he said.

"Just put them on a stick to roast them over the fire. Here are the buns. It's nice if they're toasted, too, but we don't have a grill rack."

Kolbjorn spitted the dogs on a thin twig and held it over the fire. The heavenly smell of roasted sausages filled Rachel's nostrils and made her mouth water.

"Cheers," she said, raising the bottle as if in a toast then taking a sip. The wine was good, and the rich, full taste of grapes and blackberries filled her mouth and slid down her throat, burning her stomach pleasantly. Her head began to spin almost immediately, alcohol hitting her system on an empty stomach.

She held the bottle out to Kolbjorn who shook his head curtly.

"Come on, you are a Viking," she said, "aren't you guys like big drinkers or something?"

"I am not. Never have been."

"Why not?"

"Because alcohol clouds the mind and the judgment."

"Yeah, it does. I could use some clouds in my mind right now. Plus, this is really good stuff."

"If you say so."

Rachel took another gulp and moaned, savoring the taste.

"Ah well, your loss, buddy. I fully intend to enjoy this evening because who knows, maybe I won't have another one tomorrow."

Even though she joked, the thought chilled her skin, and she chased it away. Not now. Tomorrow did not exist.

Kolbjorn watched her, and his gaze burned her skin, making her feel even more drunk.

"All these things," he said, "the sausages, the wine. When people tasted the food you left in the cart, they said it had come from Valhalla. You cannot be from Valhalla. Where are you really from?"

Rachel took another gulp. She felt careless, joy filling her chest. The most handsome man she had ever seen sat by her side roasting hot dogs. Maybe it was the alcohol talking, but she seriously considered just telling him. He had been honest with her. How badly could he really react? Maybe he would even cut her some slack. But most likely, he just would not believe her.

"I am from the future, Kolbjorn," Rachel said, and hearing the words made the corners of her mouth curl. She was much drunker than she should have been after just a few sips.

"What?"

"I am from the future. From the year 2018. Almost twelve hundred years in the future." She stared into space, considering the numbers she had just said. "Wow," she whispered.

"Don't think I believe you for a second," Kolbjorn mumbled, although he thoughtfully regarded the plastic wrapping from the hot dogs, the bottle, screw top, and then somewhere under Rachel's cloak—probably where her purse was—which made her cheeks burn.

Alcohol always made her stubborn, and proving to Kolbjorn that she was telling him the truth, became more important than anything in that moment. "You don't believe me? How do you explain this?"

She found a chocolate bar in her purse, broke the wrapping and handed it to him. "Try it. It's chocolate. Bet you never had this before. It's delicious!"

While he turned the chocolate in his free hand and sniffed at it suspiciously, she rummaged for some more evidence. She found her wallet.

"Aha!" she said, and handed him her driver's license. "Look at the date."

Kolbjorn took the card and studied it, then picked at its laminated corners. "I can see that it's a masterful portrait of you, but I don't read these runes."

"This masterful portrait is called a photo, and it's done with a machine called a camera."

His face had a blank expression. "A machine?"

"If you could read these 'runes,' you'd see that the year I was born is 1997 in the city called Chicago in the country of the United States of America."

He frowned and eyed her up and down. One of the sausages exploded into an octopus form, and he removed the stick from the fire.

"From the future..." he said with a blank stare and an intonation that suggested everything finally made sense. "The iron wasp, the food and the drinks... The goddess dancing in the air, was it one of your future tricks, too?"

"Yep. A small projector, fits in the pocket."

Kolbjorn's eyes squinted.

"Suppose I believe you. How did you travel in time then?"

"There's a golden spindle in Chicago, and when I touch it, I get sucked in and appear here. Three old ladies had it, but well"—her cheeks burned—"I stole it."

Kolbjorn froze, his eyes wide. "Three old women, a golden spindle— They are the Norns, aren't they?"

"Who?"

"Three Norns who spin people's fates. They have the power to do anything with people's lives. So it must be true. They must have sent you here."

Kolbjorn studied her. "Give it to me," he stretched his hand out for the bottle. Rachel handed it to him, surprised. "Not every day that I meet someone from the future."

He took a big sip, and once he removed the bottle from his mouth, he looked at it appreciatively and smacked his lips. Rachel wanted to kiss those lips, to feel them sucking not at the wine, but at her breasts, brushing over her skin. A tremor of warmth went through her.

He drank. "The sausages are ready." Kolbjorn waved the stick with the dogs.

Rachel reached for the pack of buns. "Put one in a bun, like this." She removed one sausage, burning her fingertips a little, and put it in a bun. "There should be ketchup and mustard in my purse." She found the small packets, ripped open the ketchup and squeezed a long line along the sausage. "Eat and repeat!"

She handed him the hot dog and he took it and almost swallowed it whole. "Mmmm," he moaned, licking his fingers. Rachel bit her lip, her mouth watering from the sight.

She made a hot dog for herself and bit into it. The juice of the sausage with a hint of woodsmoke sprung onto her tongue, and she thought she had never tasted anything so good.

"The food and the wine are from the future," Kolbjorn said, taking another sip from the bottle. "Odin would be jealous, but the Norn must be laughing at me right now! A jarl's bastard stuck in a hunting cabin with the most beautiful woman he has ever seen, and she's from another time."

Rachel's cheeks burned despite herself at his compliment. It must be the wine talking. He didn't mean what he said, but Rachel really wished that he did.

"She must be laughing at me, too, then," Rachel said, taking the bottle from him. And as their fingertips touched, their eyes locked, and Rachel's heart raced five hundred miles per hour. She couldn't remove her hand. It was as if they were glued together, as if the whole tingling world was created by their touch. "Making me care about someone I really shouldn't," she whispered.

"What?" Kolbjorn practically choked on the word.

Rachel removed her fingers, the bottle clenched in her hand. Her skin tingled where they had touched. Her lips pressed against the wet glass opening to take a sip, and she thought that this was where his lips had been just now and that it was as if they were kissing through the bottle. She closed her eyes.

"Kolbjorn, I really should not say this, but you are a great guy. If I met you in my time—"

She stopped herself before she could say too much, before she could say the words that would change everything.

But Kolbjorn's eyes burned her. From hazel they darkened to mahogany, fire dancing in them.

He shifted closer to her, and her breath caught. "Then what?"

She swallowed. "I'd be in trouble."

He shifted again, until he was sitting right next to her, and his nearness made Rachel's hands and knees weak. He brushed his knuckles across her cheek, catching a lock of her hair, and electricity tingled through her skin. "You are in more trouble than you know," he said.

He took her shoulders and pulled her to him, his mouth covering hers. Lost in the wildfire that spread through her body, she thought that he was right.

CHAPTER NINE

HIS KISS STARTED SLOW, exploring, and Rachel melted from every pull of his lips and stroke of his tongue. She ran her hands up and down Kolbjorn's chest and stomach, savoring the hardness of his muscle under his tunic.

He was kindling the fire in her, somewhere deep, making pleasure run through her like quicksilver.

Kolbjorn took control of the kiss, tilting her head back and gaining full access to her mouth. He tasted of wine and of him, and it was driving her wild.

She wanted more of him—ah hell, she wanted *everything*. How could she like him this much after having spent just a few hours with him?

The truth was, she was falling for the gorgeous Viking.

She'd been dreaming about him every night, imagining this moment since the first time she saw him. She'd been disappointed by his absence the other times she'd returned to the village, and she'd been so excited to see him again.

His smooth tongue teasing her, his teeth biting her lips playfully, his hands traveled under her cloak and brushed her back up and down, making her already-soft muscles even more pliable.

Her heartbeat drummed in her ears. Without removing her cloak, Kolbjorn undid the brooches that held the broad straps of her apron dress, and they fell heavily behind her back. He pulled the dress down to her stomach, leaving her in just a linen shift. He massaged her breasts through the fabric, and she moaned her approval into his mouth, the deepest muscles inside of her clenching.

Rachel undid the belt that held his tunic together, and let it fall lose. The leather purse thumped slightly as it fell to the floor, and Rachel registered distantly that this was where the necklace was.

But she was way too hot and way too far gone to care. She needed his big hands on her body; she needed them right on her skin. Rachel couldn't remember the last time she'd felt so strong, so sexy.

She sucked gently on his tongue, and he growled and rolled her hair on his fist—a gesture so primal it made Rachel arch her back and press herself into the hand that cupped her breast. He teased her nipple, making her rub her thighs together.

"You feel so good, Rachel," he murmured when he released her mouth to lave his tongue against her neck.

He let go of her to lift her up, apron dress hanging, and carry her to the sleeping bench, which was covered with soft furs. He undid her cloak and let it slide down her shoulders, then pulled her shift up. Fresh air, still a little chilly, bit her bare skin, and she shivered.

"I'll make you warm enough, don't you worry," he growled, undoing his own coat hastily. Then off went his linen tunic. Rachel's breath caught at the mighty sight of him.

Kolbjorn's body was all muscle. Soft curls of dark-brown

hair covered his chest, and a trail of smaller curls led beneath his waistband. Everything she had imagined in her hottest dreams come true—and then some. Silver battle scars ran across his left shoulder and his chest. Rachel's heart squeezed imagining him fighting for his father, who would never appreciate his commitment—just like her own.

She planted soft kisses on the scars, and felt him trembling under her lips.

Kolbjorn put his fur cloak around them, and the wild scent of animal mingled with leather and his own earthy essence engulfed her. He cupped her naked breasts, stroking them with the rough pads of his fingers. Then his mouth was on them, his tongue flicking her nipples, his lips torturing her skin in the sweetest way.

Rachel shook from pleasure, and she wanted to pleasure him, too. Her fingers found his rock-solid stomach and traced the soft line of curls towards the rim of his pants. She undid the rope that served as a belt and slid his trousers down his strong thighs. His erection sprang into her hand, and she bit her lip at the firm feel of it.

Kolbjorn sucked in a breath, and, encouraged, Rachel stroked his length, his skin soft and velvety under her fingertips.

But he did not let her continue. He pushed her gently so that she lay on her back, his fur cloak covering them like the wall of a cave, his mountain of a body hovering over her. Rachel wrapped her arms around his body, needing more, and he kissed her, hungrily, deeply, his tongue dipping into her mouth and dancing with hers. His lips tickled, taunted, teased her neck, the skin of her chest, then her fevered stomach, only to stoke the wildfire inside her as he continued even further down.

No one had ever done this. No one.

Not that she had much experience.

His fingers brushed her inner thighs, the rough skin at their tips making all kinds of pleasure whirl in her. Embarrassment tinged her cheeks, and she felt heat roaring within her.

For god's sake, you are not a virgin. What is wrong with you?

But she might as well have been—no one had ever kissed her *there*. And she was glad that Kolbjorn was the man she would have this first experience with.

His fingers gently dipped into the hot, damp depth of her, circling the soft, wet tissue that throbbed for attention, spurring waves of urgent pleasure, quick and fierce. But when she felt his mouth on her, fluttering against her, his soft beard intensifying every sensation, her cheeks began to burn in earnest—hell, her whole body did.

Violent pleasure was born where his tongue lashed her, and Rachel felt so wanton, so bad, and so present, her body free. As if she'd finally woken up to a world of color after years of gray.

And she did not want to go back.

Ever.

Her body was ready, her nerves saturated, sodden with pleasure.

"Kolbjorn, I'm going to come," she whimpered.

"Good," he mumbled against her.

"No," she tugged on his shoulders, so huge that her palms could only cover the tips of them. "I want you, please. I want you inside."

His head rose from between her thighs, a hungry smirk on his lips.

"As you wish."

He came up to her mouth, brushing his skin against hers, the soft hairs on his chest tickling her skin, making her burn with liquid fire.

But she wanted even more firsts tonight. She pushed him to the side slightly, and with one swift movement, turned him and was on top of him. Kolbjorn moaned in delighted surprise. His fingers came back to her sex and teased her there, then he slid one inside of her and circled, sweet pressure building up in her deep muscles.

He withdrew his fingers. "You are so wet," he whispered. "You are ready for me."

"Oh yes." A moan escaped her. "Yes."

She wriggled on top of him, burning for him and yet wanting this moment to last an eternity—the moment just before she would become his and he would become hers.

As he placed his rock-hard erection right at her entrance, their eyes locked, just like when they first saw each other in the village, and time froze, eternity connecting them. And as his hot hardness entered her, it stretched her, sending the most extreme pleasure she had ever had in her life through her muscles. Their hearts beat together, and as he began pounding into her, their movements became one.

Rachel's muscles were already clenched with pleasure, the connection between them consuming her.

Like a wave of a distant storm, her orgasm was born small and grew with each of Kolbjorn's thrusts. When he got close as well, starting to pant and then growl with every movement, the wave took her whole and broke her against the shore in a world-shattering pleasure the likes of which she had never felt. As if amplified by Kolbjorn's own release, it sent her trembling and her body moving together with his.

And as their combined breaths became one song, she thought that she had never felt so complete.

CHAPTER TEN

THE OVERWHELMING SILENCE beyond the walls of the hut crept into Kolbjorn's awareness as he slowly awakened. His body, too, felt peaceful. The house did not shake anymore, and the wind did not wail in between the slats of the hastily repaired roof. It was as if Fimbulwinter, the great winter before Ragnarok, had finally passed, and all the world lay new and quiet.

Crisp air cooled his nose and cheeks, but when he looked at the fire, he saw that it was still burning its small dance on the scorched wood. They had not slept long if the fire was still going. Despite the chill air, it was warm and cozy under his bear fur cloak.

He felt Rachel's warm, silky body spread on top of him and breathing in unison with him, and, having wrapped his arms around her, he felt that everything was right with the world.

Last night had been the highlight of his life. The woman from the future...

She was fire and love and—

He tensed, and the feeling of peace evaporated.

A thief.

He had never felt accepted by his father, and because of her, his father had cast him out completely. What was Kolbjorn thinking? That he'd bring a thief home as his woman?

How could he have been so weak? How could he have drunk her wine? He, who'd sworn to the life of sobriety because he feared doing things like this when he drank. Feared letting himself be fooled, losing control.

This was over. The storm was gone, and with it, the protective cocoon that enveloped the two of them. He had to take Rachel and the necklace to his father—the sooner, the better. He shifted to peel Rachel away from him, and she opened her sleepy eyes. Her gaze found him and she smiled, planting a kiss on his chest.

She was so beautiful, her auburn hair spread over his chest, her cheeks rosy, her lips swollen from their lovemaking and calling for him to kiss them again.

"Come back to sleep," she croaked. "I can give you space. I must be heavy."

Heavy? She was as light as a feather, and the feeling of her pressed against him was as sweet as honey. "The storm is over. We must go back."

Rachel pushed herself against him, her face paling. She knew what this meant as well as he did. She, too, had seemingly forgotten everything that existed beyond the storm, everything that put them on the opposite sides of the game.

He shifted from under her and then from under the cloak, fresh air covering his skin with goosebumps. He felt her eyes on him as he dressed.

"Are you really going to take me to your father?" she asked.

He turned to face her, and she was a sight to see—her naked, delicate shoulders peeking from under the fur, the tops of her breasts visible. The sight made his mouth dry and heat rush to his groin, but he chased the feeling away.

He had made a mistake by allowing himself to act on his attraction. There could be no future for them. She was a thief. And she belonged in a different time.

Even if Kolbjorn allowed himself to think about what would happen if she decided to stay with him, presenting a thief to his father as Kolbjorn's future wife was impossible. It went against everything the jarl wanted Kolbjorn to be. With a thief as his wife, his father would never accept him into the family. Merely considering the possibility was foolish, though, since his father would surely kill Rachel, even if Kolbjorn attempted to convince him to spare her life.

No. He must shut down his feelings towards her, feelings he never should have had in the first place. She was probably trying to manipulate him anyway.

"I am going to take you to him," Kolbjorn said, putting his clothes on. "Better get dressed."

Without throwing another glance at Rachel, Kolbjorn walked to the door. He needed to see how bad the snow was.

He opened the door a little to see, and a small drift fell inside. The snow was up to his knees. He shoved the door back into place. They could go, but the trek would be difficult.

"Do you want to have some breakfast?" Rachel said with a nervous smile. "There are still hot dogs. I can roast them."

Kolbjorn's stomach growled at the thought, but he did not want to give in to the memory of the happiest night he had ever had.

"Get dressed. We need to go."

Rachel sat upright and clutched the edges of his cloak tight around her. "Why are you being like this?"

"Like what?"

"You know like what. As if nothing happened yesterday."

He met her eyes. They were big and full of emotion. "Nothing happened yesterday," he said. "I had you as a man, like I have bed slaves and servant girls. So what?"

Rachel jerked back slightly as if he had hit her. "It was not just sex, and you know it."

He did know it. Nothing had ever come close to what he felt with her. As if every hair on his body filled with tenderness and pleasure. And not just pleasure, something more.

Completeness.

As if he'd found home.

Her.

"It was a mistake," he said. "I should not have become drunk, and I should not have— It won't change anything. I must take you to my father, and you—you must face the consequences of your actions."

Rachel paled, her eyes darting around the room as if she was looking for an answer.

"Listen," she said, when her eyes fell on her purse. "I have a solution. You don't have to take me to your father. Let me take the necklace."

Kolbjorn tensed, gripping his belt purse where the jewel lay, but Rachel held out a hand as if calming a wild animal.

"No, no, listen. Let me take it so that I can save my mother's life. In exchange, I'll bring you stuff from modern times. Valuable stuff. Food and drinks, modern jewelry with many, many gemstones. Modern technology allows us to produce stones that look just like rubies, emeralds, diamonds, at a fraction of the cost. They are almost indistinguishable to the naked eye. Your father will be so, so much richer with them than just with this necklace. He'll become a king in no time. I'll bring a lot. Look in my purse. Take the ones I have with me!"

Kolbjorn listened to her with a frown. If she told the truth, she was right, it would be a good solution. But most likely, she lied. She wouldn't come back.

"Look, look," she urged him, standing on her knees. The fur cloak slid slightly from her movement, and Kolbjorn clenched his jaws at the delicious sight of her.

Kolbjorn picked up her purse and took out a packet of the same transparent material as the bag with the sausages.

It was full of sapphires. All the exact same size, glistening in the firelight like the eyes of the Midgard Serpent. There were at least a hundred of them. He watched them, not quite believing he held such treasure in the palm of his hand.

She was right, this was much more valuable than the necklace alone.

"And these are made?"

"Yes, manufactured."

"Out of what?"

"Minerals."

"And they are cheap?"

"Yeah. Compared to the real deal. But they look almost the same."

He could not tell the difference.

"Why do you have them with you?"

"I wanted to throw them on the street so that people would fight for them, in case I was out of luck and the jeweler or the guards didn't leave the house. Take them. Just give me the Necklace of Northern Lights"—her voice broke —"and let me go," she finished in a whisper.

Kolbjorn opened the transparent purse and spilled the gemstones onto the palm of his hand. They glistened just like the real ones.

"Someday people will be able to do this?"

"Yeah."

He shook his head as if shaking off a bad dream, then put

the jewels back into the transparent purse. "You must think me a fool if you suggest that I trust your word."

Rachel frowned. "I know I seem like a thief... Well, I am. But I will come back. I swear on my mother's life."

She was in earnest. If he believed any word she had said before, nothing was more important to her than her mother. Still. He would not step from the path of honor, even for her.

"No."

Rachel scoffed and threw off the fur cloak. Her ripe breasts bounced before him, and he turned away as his cock hardened from the sight and the urge to take the beautiful flesh in his mouth, one breast after the other, until she could not withhold her moans.

As she dressed, Kolbjorn remained turned away and breathed, trying to calm down his lust.

Rachel's voice came closer, and he could hear the rustle of her pulling on clothes behind his back. "I don't understand why you must be so stubborn. I proved to you that I am from the future, and you believe me, don't you? Why can't you just trust me when I swear on the most important person in my life? What do I need to do to make you believe me?"

"I am not going back empty-handed."

"You won't! The whole pack of sapphires—there are three hundred of them!"

"Your fake gemstones won't buy my loyalty."

Rachel appeared in front of him, in her shift and her apron dress; her bare feet must have been freezing on the packed-dirt floor.

Her eyes were huge, her mouth round, her lips full. She was pleading, and he hated seeing her like this.

"Kolbjorn. Anything. Medicine, clothes, food, more gemstones. Darn it, even weapons. Ask me for anything and I'll bring it. Stuff that will make your father *beg* you to join the family. I'll be like your personal genie. Just give me the necklace and let me go."

Kolbjorn eyed her. Even if he did not want to admit it, somewhere deep, he believed her. There was nothing to prove that she'd actually go through with it, though, and he'd probably be a fool to trust her in the first place.

Did he doubt that she was from the future? No. All the things, the food, and the wine that she had—all were undeniable proof. And the Norns could do anything, even send people through time.

He needed her to stay so that he could restore his good name in front of his father.

But a huge part of him *wanted* her to stay for a whole different reason.

CHAPTER ELEVEN

"No."

Kolbjorn's voice hit Rachel like a slap across the face.

No? Just no? After everything she'd said, everything she'd offered?

She couldn't give him more. She couldn't say anything that would change his mind. He'd almost said yes, she'd seen it in his eyes, and both hope and dread had bloomed and fought inside her. Hope for her mother. Dread of separating from him.

When she had first seen him, she'd thought he was a rock. Now, she knew that with his strength and solidity came extreme stubbornness. It was freaking impossible to change his mind.

And his answer confirmed her biggest fear. She was falling for him, and he would never choose her. He'd destroy her. She had to protect herself before it was too late.

"You know what, Kolbjorn? You want to be your father's real son? The *jarl's* son, huh? So that he'll approve of you and let you make important decisions with him, and so that you'll become the next jarl? You are so fixated on your principles, on doing anything to please your father, that you can't even bend a little to do what's best for *you*. You don't see that he's using you like a dog! Because you are like a dog—you don't have your own rules; you live by your master's, your father's!"

Kolbjorn's face began to redden, and she knew she'd struck a nerve.

"Yeah. Exactly. You think that the way to please your father is by following his every command? By sacrificing everything that you are so that he'll love you and take you in? He knows that no matter what he does, you'll always be there for him! He trained you well."

"Shut up."

"Shut up? What, afraid of the truth? Let's say he accepts you as his heir, and you become the jarl. How do you plan to be a leader if everything is about honor for you? What do you do if someone threatens you with war, huh, Kolbjorn? It's just like in my world. Responding like a rigid soldier, with violence, is not always the best answer for your people. That's great for warriors—who'll most likely get themselves killed anyway. But for leaders, honor is a tool. And if you don't understand that, then you are nothing more than an instrument, there to be used and discarded at your father's will."

"You don't know anything. You are an outlander from a different time."

"No? Well, maybe not. But I do know one thing. I'd give anything to save my mother. Anything. As you see, I am ready to steal and travel through time and offer things I never thought I would—like weapons. But her life depends on me, and there's a deadline on that. Nothing you do for your father is ever enough. And it never will be. When are you going to stop living by your father's rules and start living by your own?"

Kolbjorn was white now, from rage. Oh no, she'd overdone it.

"You'd give anything for your mother?" he said. "And where is this leading you? First you took the golden spindle from three old women. Then you stole jewelry from my house —never mind that my whole life was turned upside down. Then you steal more jewelry, intended as an important gift to help my village. What next, Rachel? You are heading for the life of an outlaw, and where do you think you will stop?"

Rachel panted as his words ripped her apart. He'd hit her right where she was most vulnerable, right where she refused to look at herself—because if she did, she wouldn't be able to lift a finger anymore. And if her mother knew what she was doing for her, she'd never be able to look at her daughter the same way again. Rachel had lied, told her the money was from an anonymous benefactor, a fan of her work.

And Kolbjorn was right, she had not thought about her future beyond saving her mother. What *would* she do once her mother was well again? What would Rachel be good at?

Stealth? Theft? Deception?

She'd been so focused on taking care of her mom the past six years, she hadn't taken time to stop and think what she would actually like to do with her life.

And Kolbjorn was right, what about the consequences? How had she impacted the lives of the people she had stolen from?

How would she look her brother and her mother in the eye?

Cold sweat covered Rachel's whole body, and she only now noticed that her bare feet, standing on the packed-dirt floor, felt like cubes of ice.

And yet, she still felt that facing everything she had done and everything that was happening to her now was better than seeing her mother's coffin.

Tears welled in her eyes.

Kolbjorn's expression—even though still furious—now

held a hint of softness. The sight of him, tall, proud, and honorable, steadied her.

He was a rock, a home, a shelter. And he was right. This huge, gorgeous, infuriating man who saw through her and who pulled her closer as if by gravity. She wiped her eyes.

She was afraid to let anyone else into her heart because doing so led to world-shattering pain. Too late. That was exactly what she had done.

"If you were mine," Kolbjorn said, "I'd straighten you out even after everything you've done, like a man should straighten out his—"

Rachel's stomach clenched in a sweet ache. Silence hung between them, heavy and saturated. The smallest light of hope kindled somewhere in Rachel, making her breathe faster, sending excitement vibrating through her like a million fireflies.

The vein on his neck pulsed in the same violent rhythm as her heart. Rachel's mouth went dry. And the same pull that had always been there when they were near, and that had brought them together as powerfully as the strength of the storm, made her forget everything else.

"If I was yours— Then make me yours."

THAT WAS ALL the invitation he needed.

He went to her and scooped her into his arms, his mouth hungry.

She felt ice cold, but he'd warm her up.

He had seen in her eyes that she was redeemable after all, that his heated words had struck a chord—the hidden wound, the pain he recognized in himself.

If she was his...

She wanted this as much as he did.

They did not have a future, but that was for later. All they had was this moment. And she was in his arms.

And everything was possible.

As long as his skin was against hers—she was warm and beautiful and fiery, with all the right curves—nothing else existed.

He wanted her like he had never wanted anyone or anything else in the world.

The desire burned him from the inside, awoken like a hungry beast who needed only her. He would not be able to breathe, to move, his heart would not continue beating, if she was not his. If he could not dissolve in her.

He wanted nothing but to plunge into her tightness, but that would not be enough. He needed to savor every movement, every lick, every pull of her lips and stroke of her tongue, the fullness of her breasts and the silk of her belly...

He pulled her skirts to her waist, lifted her up, and she wrapped her legs around him, her sex pressing against his erection, the sensation making him growl.

He could not stop kissing her, savoring the taste of her, the sweet-apple smell of her hair—and that intoxicating feminine scent of Rachel that made him harden even more.

Holding her with one arm, he undid his trousers with the other hand, and his cock pressed against her bare ass, swelling even more. Rachel shifted and began rubbing herself against him, searching.

She pushed herself against him and planted herself on his erection, the slick velvety heat surrounding him and sending a tremor of pleasure through his whole body.

She was his, oh gods, she was his, this cunning beauty from another world who'd turned his whole life upside down and owned his heart from the first moment he saw her.

And he was hers.

He eased into her, gripping her ass in his hands, shafting her on his cock. Rachel's hips moved in the same rhythm, meeting his thrusts. She was so wet for him, and so tight, and the friction of their bodies moving together made him lose his mind.

"Mine," he growled, as he removed his lips from her mouth and lowered his head to plant wet, hungry kisses on her ear, her neck, and to inhale the delicious scent of her hair.

"Yes," Rachel moaned. "Yes."

The thrusts were devastating. They brought pleasure and satisfaction, and yet were not enough. Nothing was enough to make her his forever.

The waves of bliss that rocked his blood each time he set himself deeper and deeper inside of her grew like the swell of an approaching storm, making him sink faster and faster into a sea of pleasure. His thrusts became more urgent, harder, as did Rachel's cries of pleasure.

Their primal dance took them ever higher, until it felt as if their very souls connected. And as the consuming orgasm shook him in its violent waves, he felt Rachel's inner spasms milking him, intensifying every sensation and making him forget about everything outside of this moment.

Everything except the fierce, brave, beautiful woman in his hands.

He did not remember how he got her back to the sleeping bench, how he got there himself. But after the orgasm let go of him, she cuddled against him, his arms around her, and his or her whisper "Mine" was the last thing he knew before he fell asleep.

CHAPTER TWELVE

RACHEL'S BODY tingled with Kolbjorn's heavy arms around her, his chest rising and falling peacefully against her back. Her muscles felt soft, as if they had been soaked in warm chocolate. Tears welled in her eyes, and one crawled down her cheek.

This would be the only tear she'd allow herself.

Emotions battled inside her body. The tears were of happiness, of joy, of the intensity of the world-shattering, deep physical connection with the first man she'd fallen in love with.

But also of loss.

Because she was about to betray him.

Kolbjorn was asleep, the storm was over. She would go to save her mother, and also to prevent Kolbjorn from shattering her heart into a million pieces.

She was not terrified of death. But she had barely recovered when her father left, and now she was in danger of losing her mother. Losing Kolbjorn would be the end of her soul. And that was what would happen when he abandoned her, sacrificed

her, to please his father. He didn't see any other alternative—
he'd made that clear enough.

Rachel wiped her tears and gently kissed his strong arm,
which was wrapped around her shoulders.

"I'm sorry," she mouthed, and inch by inch she slid from
underneath him until her feet were on the floor. She pulled on
her shoes and slid her cloak over the dress she was still
wearing.

Something creaked outside of the house. It must have been
the wind. Perhaps another storm was coming. Daylight seeped
through the roof patchwork, only a couple of hours must have
passed since Kolbjorn had tried to open the door. She needed
to hurry to get back home before the kidney went to someone
else.

Rachel sank to the floor and, with trembling hands, opened
Kolbjorn's belt pouch and fished out the necklace. She left the
sapphires so that he would not go back to his father empty-
handed.

A soft thump against the wall made her freeze and glance
in that direction, but nothing followed. It must have been a
tree branch in the wind. Kolbjorn continued to wheeze sweetly
in his sleep. Rachel would love to crawl back onto the sleeping
bench with him and huddle against the warmth of his big
body, but it was impossible.

She threw a last glance at him, wishing she had a camera
inside of her eyes to forever have his image imprinted in her
psyche. She had been serious about coming back and
bringing him stuff, but since he did not want her to, since he
was still determined to take her to his father, she could not
risk it.

She had to leave.

Without a sound, she walked towards the door and pulled
it, but it did not move. Strange. She'd expected the snow to fall

in. Was it stuck because of the ice? She pulled it harder, but no result.

Then she heard something.

Voices from outside. Another thump against the wall from the opposite side. And another one from a third side.

Rachel pulled the door frantically. It felt as if it was blocked from outside.

Then the scent of burning reached her nose, and she saw a line of flame flick through the planks in the walls. Horror struck her like a brick.

Rachel flew to Kolbjorn and shook him. "Kolbjorn, wake up!"

He opened his eyes.

"The hut is burning!" Through panic, her lips could not move fast enough. "What are we going to do? The door is jammed!"

But Kolbjorn looked calm. His eyebrows knit together, he glanced around the room, estimating the situation. Then his gaze lingered on her and went as cold as ice. He quickly dressed.

"You were leaving." The steel in his voice made Rachel cringe. He looked in his belt purse. "Gone. Of course."

Rachel's blood turned to ice. Not because she was afraid of the threat in his voice. Not because she was inside a burning house with no way out.

But because she'd stepped over the line. There would be no way back. The last bloom of hope died.

"You won't change," he said, disappointment in his voice slashing at her like a knife. "So I won't change, either."

With one swift movement, he grabbed her purse and cut its straps with his ax. She clawed at his hands while he rummaged. But he just slapped her hands away like flies, found the necklace and put it back in his bag.

Rachel watched this as if she was in a slow-motion horror movie. She had now lost everything. The necklace, the chance to save her mother, the last thread of hope to be loved by Kolbjorn, and she was about to lose her life in the fire, too.

Horror gripped her heart. Her arms and legs felt weak, as if turned to jelly. Her lungs hurt.

Kolbjorn, however, seemed unmoved and looked collected. He walked to the door and tried to open it, jerking it with all his force. But it was clear now that something far stronger held it from the outside.

Gray smoke started swirling through the tiny slits between the wall planks, and Kolbjorn coughed.

He took the dirty rag from the makeshift pharmacy, soaked it in melted ice water from a bucket in the corner, and gave it to Rachel. "Cover your mouth and nose and breathe through it. Don't you dare say anything about the dirt."

Rachel nodded, numb from the shock and the feeling of loss. She did as he said—she knew in a far corner of her mind that he was right, that breathing through wet cloth helped to not suffocate from the carbon. But he didn't have anything for himself.

The fact that he put her wellbeing before his own melted her heart.

"We must get out." He studied the patched roof that they had worked so hard on.

"Are you thinking—"

"Yes. It's our only chance."

He stood on the same stool he had used to repair the roof just a few hours ago, except now he was removing the planks. How ironic was that.

The fire roared behind the walls around them, the smoke thickened, and Kolbjorn began coughing more. What was she doing standing like a statue? She had to help him. Rachel shook off the shock, looked for the woodcutting ax that she had made the nails with and found it behind the firewood stash. Shifting the table towards Kolbjorn, she stood on it.

Then she tied the rag behind her head so that she could use both her hands. Either she or Kolbjorn had to be all right in case the other one lost consciousness.

"What are you doing?" Kolbjorn coughed.

He'd managed to hack through the first flitch, and snow fell through the gap, fresh air rushing into the hut.

"Helping you. What does it look like?" Rachel continued hacking.

The work was harder than she had thought, but little by little, she managed to remove the second flitch while Kolbjorn got to the third. It was getting warmer in the room, and Rachel began to sweat.

Kolbjorn was coughing non-stop now, and she was afraid that he'd burned his lungs from inhaling too much smoke. But more fresh air came in as the gap grew larger, and soon it was big enough for them to get out.

Kolbjorn stood on the table and put Rachel on his shoulders, helping her to get onto the roof. The walls were burning, but the roof was completely untouched—a thick layer of snow covered it in soft drifts. She turned and gave Kolbjorn a hand to get out.

When Kolbjorn stood by her side, Rachel looked around. By the door, through the thick gray smoke, she saw people.

Kolbjorn said, "I'll go first, then I'll catch you," and jumped down into the snow, a lot of which had already melted from the heat of the fire.

Rachel first threw the ax into the snow, then jumped. Her breath caught, but the hut wasn't tall. And when the heat biting at her skin was left behind, and Kolbjorn's steady hands caught her, she finally exhaled a breath she didn't realize she'd been holding.

"There are people—"

"I know. My father's legitimate sons. The man who tried to kill me at the jeweler's is the eldest of my half-brothers, and he must have seen what direction I went. I can only imagine what lies they told my father."

Rachel swallowed a hard knot.

"Okay, they did not see us, let's go."

"Oh, I am not running. Stay back. This is between me and them."

CHAPTER THIRTEEN

KOLBJORN'S HEART thumped in his chest, his pulse drumming in his ears. His lungs burned from inhaling the smoke, his muscles already tired from the strain of hammering at the roof for what felt like an eternity.

He walked towards them without hiding, and as he emerged from the corner of the burning, roaring building, he saw Alfarr, Ebbe and three other warriors. They would have known that Kolbjorn would not get far in the storm, and this was the only shelter close to his father's village.

Kolbjorn's blood boiled. The maggots had the audacity to try to kill him—of course, like the cowards they were, stabbing him in the back, not brave enough to face him. And now there were five against one.

Rachel was right, he'd be useless as a jarl with his code of honor, with the rigidness of his beliefs. He was only as good as a pawn in the game of hnefatafl, just a warrior to execute the orders of the jarls and kings who had cunning and who could manipulate and backstab.

Such as these two.

He recognized the warriors standing by his halfbrothers: Ulf, Garpr, and Haki. He had raided with them since they had joined his father's raiding force a few years ago. They had never been friends, but he had trusted them in battle.

Now he had to fight them because his father had believed his sons, the two snakes who had wanted Kolbjorn dead ever since they were able to tell a sword apart from an ax.

These men were fresh, and he was tired. They were fully armed in battle armor, with shields, swords, axes, and scramasaxes. He only had his ax.

Odin, will this be the day I meet you?

It would be not a bad death, with his ax in his hand, fighting his true enemies.

But then—

The blood stood still in his veins, his breath froze in his lungs, and he staggered a moment.

If he died, what would they do to Rachel?

The memories of how Alfarr behaved with women during raids made his skin crawl.

No. He could not die. At least not until Rachel was out of danger from them. How ironic. He was doing everything now to save her life, yet if he succeeded he'd still take her to his father.

He glanced back and saw her, wide-eyed, staring at him, steam pumping out of her mouth in a quick rhythm.

"Run," he threw back. "Run, Rachel. Go home to your mother."

"I'm not leaving you. If they injure you or worse—maybe I can help."

"Run."

But she stubbornly shook her head, and it both pleased him and made sweat break through his skin from fear for her.

Let it be then. The Norn had put another stitch in the tapestry of his life. His woman wanted to stand by him—To all goblins, why was he thinking of her as *his* woman?—and he'd rather die than let harm come to her.

He touched Mjölnir—Thor's hammer—on his pendant, calling for the protection of the god of battle who had never left him, never let him lose a single fight.

"Thor!" he yelled as he launched himself like a spear at his enemies.

He roared as he ran—no, clambered—through knee-deep snow, calling the holy battle fury. One against five. The fury and the ax were all he had now.

It was hard to run in snow and would be hard to fight in it. But there was the burning house, and it could be his ally or his biggest enemy.

They clashed, the three warriors against one, Alfarr and Ebbe standing behind, of course, letting others do their dirty work.

Ulf was scything an ax towards his face, but Kolbjorn pierced his shoulder and kicked him into the fire, and his agonized scream was lost in the roar. Garpr hit Kolbjorn with his shield from the side. Kolbjorn staggered and almost fell but whirled, the blade of his ax cutting off the man's foot. He fell, and Kolbjorn caught Garpr's shield to protect himself—a mistake. Haki slashed Kolbjorn's upper arm with his sword, the pain hitting him like a lightning bolt.

He heard Rachel's scream and cursed because he was sure that Alfarr and Ebbe had heard her, too.

Kolbjorn whirled around and went for Haki, ax hammering, but only hit the shield, splinters scattering from under his blade. His wounded arm was weakening—he'd normally have split the wood by now.

He allowed his eyes to dart towards his half-brothers and saw that only Alfarr stood there.

Worry kicked his gut like a boot. Ebbe must be hurrying to Rachel. Gods, he hoped she hid or ran away now.

He had to get to Ebbe before he got to her.

Kolbjorn roared and came at Haki, hammering at him like a blacksmith, and one thrust found its aim, splitting the shield in two...and with the next hit, the man's head. Blood sprayed in a fountain, and the man sank to his knees and then fell to his side in the snow.

Kolbjorn twisted, his eyes searching for Ebbe and Rachel, but they were nowhere to be seen.

Alfarr was coming at him now, one eye black on the side that Kolbjorn had hit yesterday. Alfarr aimed for Kolbjorn's wounded arm—of course he did, the contemptible worm—but Kolbjorn escaped the sword and hit Alfarr from behind with his shield.

He could not kill his half-brother. Even though he deserved death for all he had done, Kolbjorn knew that his father would be devastated, and he could not bring such pain to him.

But Alfarr was not a bad warrior, and he thrust his sword, almost piercing Kolbjorn's shoulder. Kolbjorn dodged and smashed the man with the back of his ax.

"Afraid to spill my blood, mongrel?" Alfarr growled as he beat Kolbjorn's shield down and plunged his sword into the empty space between Kolbjorn's arm and body, just missing his rib.

"I am not afraid of you," Kolbjorn spat as he kicked at Alfarr. His brother had to take a step back to avoid falling down. Seeing an opportunity, Kolbjorn slashed Alfarr's thigh, and blood spilled like red lightning.

Alfarr fell on one knee, clutching at his leg and screaming.

Kolbjorn left him and clambered through the snow looking for Rachel.

The house roared with fire, the earth black around it, and dark clouds of smoke billowed into the white sky.

Behind the house, he saw broad tracks and a chill reached his bones. He rushed towards the sound as fast as he could, ramming through snowdrifts, his heart beating war drums in his ears.

Then he saw them.

Ebbe by the tree and Rachel several feet above him, plastered to the tree trunk, hugging it like a ship's mast. Ebbe cursed and hit the trunk with his ax, but he had no spear and no bow to reach her.

"Get away, Ebbe, you rotten fish's turd!" Kolbjorn roared.

Their heads shot in his direction. Ebbe paled and ran.

Kolbjorn pressed on after Ebbe, but the man was as quick as a bird. He was unharmed and had not just fought four men.

When Kolbjorn knew that he would not be able to reach his half-brother, he stopped, hands on his knees, steam rushing from his mouth and clouding his vision. His lungs burned from the smoke and from the strain of the fight. He allowed himself a fit of coughing that tore his throat and chest apart.

"Loki's sweaty ass," he mumbled when the cough subsided.

"Are you all right?" Rachel called out.

She began crawling down, carefully, cursing. "Who knew that coming down from a tree would be harder than climbing it," she said. "Are you okay?"

Finally, she jumped down, awkwardly, and sank into the snow right on her ass. He helped her up.

"You're wounded! Let me see." She turned him to see his arm.

"It's nothing."

"We need to get someone to look at it. It's not nothing. You're bleeding a lot."

He turned to look at his arm.

"I've had worse. Let's go. We need to take Alfarr with us. I can't leave him here. He's bleeding much more than I am."

They clambered to the front of the hut. Alfarr lay in the snow, which was crimson around him. The three warriors were all dead. Rachel gasped, her hand shooting to her mouth. "We need to tie his hip to stop blood loss," she mumbled through her hands.

Kolbjorn glanced at her. She was as pale as the snow, her eyes wide. She looked like someone who had seen death for the first time.

"Yes. Let me." He sank on his knees and tore the edge of her apron dress to make a bandage, then bound Alfarr's leg as best he could. They needed to hurry. Alfarr had lost a lot of blood, his skin grayish and clammy.

"We need to make a sledge. There's no way I can carry him home through the snow. I'll cut pine tree branches broad enough to put him on."

"I'll help," she said, hefting the woodcutting ax.

Kolbjorn met her eyes, and relief at seeing her unharmed flooded him. Her beautiful face spread in a broad smile that made the whole day brighter, and he could not see anything else but her.

No. Thief. She had betrayed him, stomped on all the hope that he had been stupid enough to feel. He had been right all along. He needed to shove his feelings far away. They had no future, and he had better remember that.

She grabbed his arm, and tingling went through him. "I'm so glad you're okay," she whispered, her lips trembling.

His solar plexus and his chest were on fire, torn between

his duty to his father and his love for the woman who had threatened everything that had been important to him.

"Don't be. Nothing has changed. You betrayed me. You have been playing games with me all along. But no more. It's over."

CHAPTER FOURTEEN

THE TREK down the hill went better than he had expected, but it was still difficult. They were not on skis, and snow crept into every crease of Kolbjorn's boots and trousers.

He pulled the sledge bearing an unconscious Alfarr behind him. Rachel had offered to help, but she wouldn't be able to.

His arm hurt more and more, as if fire now burned in his wound as well.

The world was still and white around them, the only sound the crunch of snow accompanying each step as their legs sank into the snowdrifts.

Kolbjorn could not stop watching Rachel. He told himself that he needed to make sure she was all right. The truth was, he was enjoying the sight way too much. Rachel panted, her cheeks now deliciously pink from the frost, her hair dark against the snow. The sight of her, flushed like that, reminded him of what he did to her with his hands and his cock, and despite himself, a surge of desire went through him.

They did not speak.

What was there to say? He was taking her to his father, she knew that.

He wondered what she was thinking just now. Was she plotting her escape? He doubted she'd give up if she had even the slightest chance.

And what would Father do once they got there?

Kolbjorn knew how the jarl dealt with thieves: he slit their throats. Never had he made anyone an outlaw, which was an even worse punishment. An outlaw lived outside of society and anyone could lawfully kill them...or do anything else they saw fit.

Anything.

Kolbjorn swallowed a hard knot. He imagined Rachel on her knees, his father's hand gripping her hair, his scramasax at her gentle white throat. Agony raged in his gut from the image, making him want to howl.

The world without Rachel.

His skin crawled at the thought, the burning in his lungs and throat agonizing, as if a swarm of angry wasps was stinging him from the inside.

Rachel was right, he was too rigid. Was there something else he could do that would let him save her, allow his father to have the necklace, and save her mother?

Could he really just let Rachel go?

Could he say to his father that she'd run away but he had the necklace? She'd be gone. The thought planted anguish in his gut twisting his insides like a woman twisting laundry.

He would be a liar then, but at least she'd be alive.

He opened his mouth to say something, but Rachel stopped and said, "Who are they?"

The village was just down the hill—he could already see the dark walls of the houses. And the sacred grove stood a short distance before them. In front of it were people on skis.

Kolbjorn moved next to her in a protective stance.

"That would be my father and his men," he said, feeling as if a boulder was sinking in his gut.

RACHEL FROZE, feeling as if she was lying trapped on a train track and the train was bearing down on her at full speed.

"I can still run," she choked out. "Cover me. Let me go."

"It's too late," Kolbjorn said, his voice barely audible. "He's seen you now."

Her feet refused to move, but having Kolbjorn next to her felt strangely reassuring. He had just saved her from the fire and from his brother. Would he save her from his father?

The men on skis approached, dogs barking around them. There were twelve men, all with spears, swords, and shields. The sight of so many weapons made Rachel's throat clench like a fist. She had never seen the promise of death so close.

Jarl Bjorn stood in front of the rest. Rachel had only seen him once, at a distance, but he was a man that you did not forget. He was every image the word "Viking" conjured: blond, long haired, and stoic, with a straight back, broad shoulders, and as much might as three modern men combined.

Chills went down her spine, and she felt small under his piercing gaze. The eyes of someone who had ruled the lives and the deaths of many looked at her, and in them was her destiny. It didn't look good.

Ebbe, covered in snow and panting, stood by his father's side.

"See, Father! He almost killed Alfarr!"

Jarl Bjorn's eyes shot to the sledge behind Kolbjorn, and his eyebrows knit together, hidden worry distorting his proud face.

"Is he alive?" he asked.

"He is, but he needs help, and now," Kolbjorn said.

Jarl Bjorn gave a sideways nod, and three men rushed to him and slid the sledge with Alfarr towards the village.

"Is this true? You almost killed him?" said the jarl.

"Yes. Because your sons tried to kill me—they set the hunting hut on fire, where I hid from the storm."

"Ebbe saw you and her, the woman who stole everything. We know you were behind it all. I sent them."

Rachel stifled a gasp. Kolbjorn took the news with a raised chin, hurt flickering in his eyes for a fraction of a second. His hand gripped the leather purse on his belt.

"Your sons are treacherous worms. Alfarr came after me, secretly, trying to kill me, making it look like I was the one behind it all." He looked straight at his father. "And it looks like they succeeded."

Jarl Bjorn shifted. "I did not say I believed them."

"But you sent them to burn us."

"I asked them to find you, the thief, and the necklace. I did not know if you survived the snowstorm," he said, his voice breaking. "Where is the necklace?"

Kolbjorn clenched his jaw and looked at Rachel with a fierce heat mixed with worry, and her body buzzed with hope. An unspoken message ran between them. Everyone and everything ceased to exist, just him and her. She was asking him to choose her. She tried to recreate the same pull they had both felt the first moment their eyes locked, as if she was a witch, a magician, and she could accomplish this just by wishing.

But the fire died in his eyes, and she knew even before he removed the necklace from the purse that she had failed. Her chest tightened and hurt as if clenched by a vice. She'd lost him. He'd lost the battle with himself.

He'd chosen his father.

The necklace glimmered in his hands, pure gold with interwoven branches, the bodies of beasts and snarling dragons, and among them, Freyja, the goddess of the North. The necklace was so delicate, as if made of golden lace, the details of the faces, eyes, bodies so precise it seemed as if they had just frozen for a moment and would begin to move at any time. Rubies, emeralds, and diamonds decorated the beasts' eyes, Freyja's crown of flowers, the fur trim of her clothes. They were big and small, and Rachel knew, now that she saw it in full daylight, that the auctioneer was right—it would easily go for a hundred thousand, and probably much, much more.

It was breathtaking.

But more importantly, it would save her mother.

The gold and the gemstones were the only color against the whiteness that surrounded them, and everyone's eyes were glued to Kolbjorn's hand.

Rachel glanced at the sacred grove, just twenty feet away. She could even see the rock. Could she grab the necklace and dart for it? Could she reach it in time? It hadn't worked last time, so she might be sentencing herself to a quick death by a Viking's ax.

She'd already tensed, adrenaline rushing through her body, preparing for her launch.

But Bjorn's hand grabbed the necklace, and it disappeared under the folds of his cloak.

Disappointment and desperation flooded her as if she was sinking into a pool of boiling lava. It quickly chilled and froze her in place when she met the jarl's eyes.

They were cold and furious.

"I see, Kolbjorn, that you are not a traitor. You delivered both the necklace and the thief."

Rachel's stomach knotted like those snarling beasts' bodies. His eyes promised death.

"I do not forgive those who make me look like a fool in front of a king. And especially those who threaten my chance to become one."

He took a step towards Rachel and grabbed her arm. She shrieked, horror stiffening her whole body. She jerked her arm, trying to get away, to get anywhere but here.

But the scramasax already glistened in the jarl's hand, and he turned her with one swift, practiced movement, until her back was to him and she faced Kolbjorn and the warriors, making her sink into the snow on her knees at the same time.

"Let this be known. There is no forgiveness for thieves in my jarldom. Tell everyone what happens to those who take what's mine."

The icy, sharp blade pressed against Rachel's throat, and she felt her pulse beating violently against it.

She struggled against him, trying to fight for her life, but his arm around her shoulders might as well have been steel. The blade bit at her skin the more she struggled.

This was it. Death came for her, punishment reached her.

"I'm so sorry, Mom," she whispered, tears blurring her vision. But even through them, she saw Kolbjorn.

At least she'd die looking into the eyes of the man she loved. At least she'd experienced, in her short and stupid life, how it felt to love a man and share a brief but intense moment of happiness with him.

Kolbjorn watched her, his face a mask of terror and anguish.

It's okay, she wanted to tell him. *I'm okay.*

Jarl Bjorn lifted the blade to the side to make the slit that would open her throat, and Rachel prepared for the last moment of her life.

CHAPTER FIFTEEN

"Stop!"

Kolbjorn heard himself yell the word that had been screaming in his head. He had to stop this. Seeing Rachel about to die broke something in him. He could not live with himself if he allowed his father to kill the woman he loved.

She had to live even if it meant betraying his father. She had to live even if it meant breaking the code of honor he had lived by his whole life. She had to live even if it meant his father would never accept Kolbjorn, even if he'd kill him, even if he'd make him an outlaw.

Father looked at him, annoyed by the interruption. "What? Why?"

Kolbjorn's forehead prickled with sweat. He'd never had to lie, never had to trick anyone. This was new, and Rachel had been so right when she'd said he could not achieve everything with his honor.

Sometimes he had to be a trickster, too.

And so he was—at least, trying to.

"Stop, Jarl. She's a witch. You are making a mistake by killing her."

"Why?"

The experience of lying was completely new to him, and he searched for believable explanations.

"There's more treasure where she is from."

Rachel's eyes widened, her face pale. He was proud of her; she took death like a warrior would—stoically, head held high, without begging, without humiliating herself.

"What are you talking about?"

"The iron wasp, the food and drinks, the goddess in the air —it's all her doing. She's a witch. She tricked us with magic."

Bjorn only gripped her stronger. "Yes, she's a witch, and she has to die. Even a volva does not get to steal from me and live."

Loki, god of mischief, help me. Sit on my shoulder, whisper to me the words that would save the woman I love.

He did not know if Loki heard his prayer or not, but somehow, the lie was born in his head.

"But she can bring more treasure. Treasure that is worth five times more than the Necklace of Northern Lights."

The jarl squinted at Kolbjorn. "Can you prove that?"

Kolbjorn nodded and removed the transparent pouch with the sapphires from his belt purse. They glimmered even brighter against the snow. He came closer to his father, the gemstones in his opened palm. Father removed the scramasax from Rachel's throat, and Kolbjorn began breathing easier. The jarl took the pouch and rustled the material between his fingers. He dipped one finger into the pouch and circled it.

"They feel real. Why do you steal my jewelry if you have these, witch?" he asked Rachel.

"She likes jewelry—she's addicted to it. She has raw materials but not this beauty, the artful jewelry that you commissioned."

"But why steal? Why could you not trade instead?"

"Because Loki is her god, and he told her to do mischief," Kolbjorn said.

Spinning lies was hard for him. Harder than fighting and killing ten men. Every word was like a wet, slippery stone in a stream, and he had to choose very carefully where he stepped.

Father looked at him long and hard, his eyes squinted, probing. Kolbjorn did not look away, sweat streaming down his spine. Father would know. He'd see the lies in Kolbjorn's face. He knew him like no one.

But his father nodded and looked down at Rachel. "It is hard to believe, but I have never heard a lie from you, Kolbjorn. If you say it is so, then it is. And if there is more treasure, then I must have it. What do you say, witch, your life for more of this?"

He dangled the pouch and it rustled.

Rachel nodded, and a cloud of steam puffed out of Kolbjorn's mouth. His first lie to Father. He felt as dirty as Loki's sweaty armpit, but Rachel was still breathing, and that was what mattered.

Now he had to get her back to her time—with the jewel.

"She needs the necklace."

"What?"

"For the spell," Kolbjorn said. "Or it won't cast."

Jarl Bjorn regarded her, heavily, and Kolbjorn thought that he'd say no and grab her again. And this time he wouldn't let her go.

Bjorn glanced at the sapphires. One hand went under the folds of his cloak and removed the necklace, but still he did not give it to her.

"How can you prove you will be back with more treasure?"

RACHEL SWALLOWED. She reached under her own cloak, to the silver necklace around her neck. She undid the clasp, removed it and held it out in her palm for Bjorn to see, her hand shaking. Separating from the necklace was like separating from her mother, from her childhood, from an integral part of herself.

"It's my mother's," the words came out in a pained whisper.

Bjorn regarded it, then took it and turned it in his hand. "This is just silver. It does not stand close to the Necklace of Northern Lights."

"But it means everything to me. I'll be back for it." She stole a glance at Kolbjorn, who watched her with such intensity, she thought he'd set her skin on fire.

Jarl Bjorn gave a nod and placed the Necklace of Northern Lights in Rachel's hands. Rachel felt as if a piece of her heart was left with her silver necklace in his hand, but if it was the price for her mother's life, then so be it.

Still shaking, her back tense, her shoulders aching as if a vise gripped them, Rachel stumbled through the snow towards the grove and the rock that appeared black against the whiteness. She felt the jarl's heavy eyes on her. "Be back tomorrow," he called after her, and she almost flinched. "Jul is in a week."

"Tomorrow," she said, breathing deeper to steady her shaking breath. That was a lie, and she did not even want to look at Kolbjorn.

She continued, and Kolbjorn went with her. The rest of the warriors together with Jarl Bjorn followed.

She was well aware of Kolbjorn's tall frame walking by her side, and even though it could not physically be possible, it felt as if his presence warmed her.

She still could not believe that Kolbjorn had lied for her, that he'd tricked his father for her.

He'd chosen her.

Warmth spread through her whole body, joy bubbling in her stomach.

He'd listened. He would not play by his father's rules anymore.

The realization made Rachel smile, but she hid it, too afraid to do anything that would make Bjorn doubt her.

Kolbjorn's face was a stone mask, his eyebrows knit together, his eyes staring in front of him but not seeing. He looked stiff and tense. Did his shoulders hurt, too?

The rock with the runes was very close when Rachel finally started believing that she was actually going, that the necklace was in her hand, that she was alive, and that she was leaving Kolbjorn.

The fear and the adrenaline that had flooded her body for the past day, and especially in the past few hours, were gone.

She was about to lose Kolbjorn forever. A sucking, ripping tornado of pain began whirling somewhere in her middle. She put a hand on her stomach in a useless attempt to calm it down.

He was still next to her, and then they were in front of the rock.

Only about a third of the pillar was visible, a cap of snow on top of it. And even though Rachel wanted to go—needed to go—the rock that she had almost fought for with her life just yesterday now looked like the promise of doom.

She turned to face Kolbjorn.

Steam rushed out of his mouth and nose in a fast, unsteady rhythm. His hazel eyes were serious. He looked like he wanted to say something but held himself back.

Rachel had to go, there was no way she could stay now.

And even if her mother was fine, Rachel did not belong here, not in this time.

Not with him.

Or did she?

Rachel swallowed. Looking at Kolbjorn, big and gorgeous and kind, her heart started to bleed. She'd fallen for him, so deeply she wasn't sure there was a bottom.

But no. She couldn't wait another minute, not with so many Vikings staring at her, their axes and swords sharp, their faces mistrustful.

And she couldn't stay another minute because with every moment that passed, it was harder and harder to leave him, the whirlwind of pain in her gut turning faster and consuming more and more of her.

Rachel leaned into Kolbjorn, her lips finding his, planting a last desperate kiss on him despite everyone looking. He answered, his arms wrapping around her, squeezing her against him in a bone-crushing hug.

"I love you," she whispered, wetting his ear with her tears.

Then without meeting his eyes, she pushed herself off him, and he let her go. She turned to the rock, putting her hands on its rough surface, sinking them in snow, the ice burning her hands.

And as the feeling of spinning began, pulling her in, she turned to see Kolbjorn for the last time. The world began disappearing, until all she could see were his eyes, just like that first time they had met, eternity connecting them even as darkness began taking everything around her.

And then there was nothing.

CHAPTER SIXTEEN

CHICAGO, DECEMBER 24, 2018

CHRISTMAS TREE LIGHTS sparkled in the darkness of the evening in Rachel's backyard. Rachel, Mom and James sat around a makeshift campfire roasting hot dogs and marshmallows, their highly unusual but fun Christmas Eve dinner.

A feeling of gratitude spilled in Rachel's chest as she glanced at her mom's healthy blush and James's concentrated face. All thanks to Kolbjorn.

"Mom, do you want more tea?" Rachel reached out for the thermos that stood by her camping chair.

"No, Rachel, I'm okay." Kendra pulled the edge of the quilt that covered her closer to her chest. She'd gained weight and color had come back to her face. Her eyes were shining again, and last week she'd even insisted on having her hair dyed red—Rachel had done if for her, just like before.

"Are you cold?" Rachel leaned forward, about to go grab another blanket or help her mom get up to go inside.

"I'm great. Making a campfire, cooking hot dogs and s'mores for Christmas, was such a great idea, honey."

James removed the stick with steaming hot dogs from the fire and placed them on the plate in his lap.

"Who wants another one?"

"Me!" Kendra said, and Rachel frowned.

"Should you have so many hot dogs?"

Her mother only waved her hand and took the bun from James's hands. "I'm having a blast," she said through a mouthful. "I feel like I'm whole and well again. I think tomorrow will be the day I go into my smithy."

"That's great, Mom!" James said, biting into a hot dog.

Rachel smiled. Maybe Mom was ready to start working, just a little bit. "I'll Be Home for Christmas" played from James's smartphone speaker in the background. Rachel took a deep breath, calm filling her. She leaned back in her chair and closed her eyes, breathing in the smell of roasted hot dogs, woodsmoke, and red wine.

The scent that would always remind her of the man she'd never see again. The man she craved more than her next breath.

Kolbjorn.

A bit over three months had passed since the surgery, three months of hope, of worry, and of the anguish that had planted its roots in Rachel's heart the day she'd left Kolbjorn. Every day since then, Rachel had been torn between the joy of seeing her mother recovering well and the loss of leaving the man she loved behind. She often found herself staring into space, thinking of Kolbjorn, feeling that something significant was lacking in her life, that she had lost a part of her soul somewhere along the way.

And she knew exactly where.

In ninth century, Norway.

Now, Mom was fine—the kidney was working. James who had always been skilled with IT had graduated from school early and would start a new job in January as a junior web developer while doing an online college degree. Even though Rachel had insisted he should apply to do a full-time degree and just study, he'd said that he was grown enough to earn money, and that she was not the only one who wanted to support the family. That it was time he gave back.

Rachel respected his decision, even though she did not agree. But she knew she did not need to babysit him any longer. He'd be all right.

"I'm going to bed," James said.

"Code word, 'girlfriend video-chat,' " Rachel teased with a smile.

James blushed. He stood up, kissed Mom on the cheek and tousled Rachel's hair on the way to the house.

"You are still such a kid," Rachel called after him, straightening her hair.

After he left, Rachel felt her mom's eyes on her. "What?"

"Do you have someone to video-chat with?"

Rachel's cheeks burned. How could Mom be so intuitive?

"No," she said.

It was true, technically. It would be impossible to video-chat with Kolbjorn. But Rachel knew what Mom meant.

"But I do have someone I care about."

"I knew those blank stares on the verge of tears meant something. Who is he? Is he the one who connected you with the anonymous philanthropist who paid for the surgery?"

Rachel felt unwelcome tears burning her eyes. "He helped. Yes."

"Well, where is he? Can I meet him?"

How was she supposed to answer that? "I don't think so, Mom."

"Tell me about him."

Tell her about Kolbjorn. Where did she even begin? "He's drop-dead gorgeous. And strong. And so stubborn." She chuckled, wiping her tears. "And he has the biggest heart. I never met anyone like him, and I never will again. We had this connection. Like, earth-stopping, star-shooting, heart-stabbing connection. And without him, you wouldn't be here."

Rachel wouldn't be here either, but she did not tell this to her mother. Mom looked at her with tenderness and smiled.

"I never had anything like that with your dad," Kendra said.

Rachel straightened. "What?"

"I loved him, but nothing like you describe. That man sounds really special, Rach. Why can't you be together?"

Rachel opened her mouth to answer—because she needed to be here, in this time, to make sure her mother was fine, to make sure they had money, to take care of James... But looking at Mom smiling, eating hot dogs, and planning to work tomorrow, Rachel wasn't sure anymore if the family really needed her so much. James was going to work and study. Everything looked like Mom would finally be fine.

But what about Rachel, would she be?

"We can't be together because—"

But the only reason that came to mind was that Rachel did not have the spindle anymore.

When she had come back with the necklace, the spindle had been gone. And no matter how hard Rachel looked, it was not there.

"Because of me?" Kendra said. "Sweetie, I'm fine. You've done everything—everything—for me, and more. You can live a little."

Rachel choked out a happy laugh.

"Mom, you do not stand in the way of my happiness. It's a bit more complicated."

"What's complicated?"

"I—I don't have a way to find him."

"Ah. But if you did?"

Rachel thought about it. If she had the spindle, what would she do? Would she really go back in time to Kolbjorn, abandon her family, the conveniences of modern life, the luxurious security of the society she lived in? And what about Jarl Bjorn, who had wanted her dead?

And surprisingly easily, an answer bubbled up in her heart.

"Yes," she said. "In a heartbeat."

Mom smiled. "Then you should find a way."

"But what if it would require me to never see you or James again? What if it would mean I won't even be able to talk to you?"

Mom frowned. "What? Why?"

"I can't explain. But what if? Would you still want me to go and find that man?"

Mom leaned over and took Rachel's hands in hers. Mom's palms were warm, and they enveloped Rachel's and made her feel better.

"Sweetheart, when I made your father leave—"

"What?"

Kendra sighed. "Yeah. I'm sorry. I've never told you this because I didn't want you to hope for something that would never happen. I made him leave. He became involved in organized crime, and I could not have him around you anymore. I made him leave, and when you assumed he'd abandoned you, I never corrected you because I didn't want you to look for him. I wanted to protect you and James. I felt terrible. It broke my heart that you started hating your dad, but that was better than risking your life."

"He didn't choose to leave. You made him?"

The realization hit Rachel like a train. Her mind raced, recalling all the times she'd cried over him, all the times she'd promised herself not to care about anyone anymore, all the times she'd wondered why her father had decided he no longer wanted the three of them. And how she was terrified of letting new people in because she might lose them one day. Most of all, she'd been afraid of letting Kolbjorn into her heart. But he hadn't abandoned her. He'd chosen her.

"Yes," Mom said. "I did not want you to be in danger because of him, and I didn't want you to learn about crime."

Too late for that, Rachel thought, guilt hanging in her chest like a rock.

"So there was no abandonment," Rachel said out loud. "It was protection."

"It was, honey."

Rachel thought that she needed to be angry with her mother—why hadn't she told her this before? But Rachel had never told her what she'd done and how far she'd gone to save her life.

She did not need to fear loving anymore. Something inside of her healed. And it felt like all was right in the world, except for one thing.

No amount of modern conveniences or the closeness of her family—no matter how much she loved them—made up for the fact that Rachel's life would never be complete without the man who owned her heart and soul.

And even though the chance of finding a way back to him was microscopic, she had to take it.

Her mission had been fulfilled here. She could go.

She couldn't live with herself if she didn't try to see if her happiness lay more than a thousand years in the past, with a Viking.

"You're right, Mom," Rachel said, jumping to her feet. "I do need to find him."

"Where? In Tajikistan?"

Rachel laughed. "Something like that. Would you still want me to do it? Knowing that I'd be happy with him, but you won't see me anymore?"

"Can you guarantee that he is not a criminal?"

"I guarantee," Rachel said, smiling. A criminal Kolbjorn was not—not for a Viking, anyway. With bitterness, Rachel thought of the irony...that *she* was the criminal. She hoped her mom would never learn the truth about how her operation was funded. And yet, Rachel would do it all over again if she had to.

Kendra's eyes filled with tears. "I understand," she said, nodding. "I still would, honey. When you are a mother, it's really hard to let your children go. But you are so grown up. You were a mother to me for the past six years. And you saved my life. I'll miss you every second, Rachel, but you do need to live your own life. You can't live it for me. You need to live it for you."

Rachel grasped her mother in a tight hug. "Mom, I love you so much."

"I love you, too. And I'll wait for you every day of my life, but knowing that you are happy and well is all I need."

Rachel stayed a bit longer with her mom, enjoying her company, and thinking that she had just gotten the most precious gift for Christmas. She could go to Kolbjorn. If all went well, this would be her last Christmas with her family, probably ever, and she wanted to savor every moment.

After Mom and Rachel extinguished the fire and cleaned up, Rachel went to her room, a fluttering in her chest like a scarf on the wind. She looked around the room that had been her oasis her whole life—the lilac walls with posters of soccer stars; the door-post with the markings of her height as she was growing up; the desk with her dad's old laptop, as thick and heavy as a briefcase. There were photo frames with pictures of the four of them camping together—one of the happiest days of Rachel's childhood—before Dad had left and before Mom had become sick. Rachel should take them with her.

She sat on her bed, brushing her fingers across the silver quilt that her mom had sewn for her, with "Rachel" embroidered on it in gold, the letters just like the ones on her necklace. She might take it with her, too. Her heart squeezed in a dull ache at saying goodbye to her life.

Tears welled in her eyes, and yet a smile spread on her face at the thought of the future with Kolbjorn that awaited her... she hoped.

After a while, wiping her tears, she opened the laptop, which took at least five minutes to load, and began searching for places the Norns could be hiding in this day and age in Chicago.

CHAPTER SEVENTEEN

"It is a rare day that a man gets a new son." Jarl Bjorn's voice rang across his mead hall at the Jul festival.

The hum of the feast died away, and even the king who sat by his side was listening.

The day after Rachel had left, Father had realized that this was the first time Kolbjorn had tricked him. Kolbjorn remembered his father staring at him as if seeing him for the first time.

After having received three hundred sapphires, Eirik gladly became Father's new official ally.

Jarl Bjorn continued, "And it's even more rare when that son is a grown man. But only when the gods had a hand in it, is that son saga-worthy. Today is my lucky day, as Kolbjorn, whom many of you know as my bastard, will join the wolves of my clan and become part of this family."

Kolbjorn had been feasting in the middle of the hall with Modolfr and his sword-brothers, listening half-heartedly to their banter, as all he could hear was the "I love you" said by the auburn-haired thief before she disappeared and took his heart with her.

He did not even register the meaning of his father's words at first. Then he felt all eyes in the hall on him like probing fingers, and he looked around and finally understood—really understood—what the jarl had said.

The words he had been yearning to hear his whole life.

Kolbjorn jumped up, his face as stiff as a stone mask, his fists clenching. He opened his mouth to say the speech that he had rehearsed so many times in his head over the years.

But nothing came.

Finally, he could feel accepted, be part of the family, be loved by his father. But those things were not important anymore.

What was important was that he was true to himself.

The realization hit him harder than his father's words.

All he'd needed all along was this inner strength, inner approval to live by his own rules. No one would be able to take it away from him. Not if he was a bastard, not if he was a jarl's son, and not if he was a jarl himself.

And as long as he had that, he'd be all right.

Kolbjorn took too long to respond to Bjorn's announcement, and his father's face looked livid. The king watched him with amusement, and Ebbe looked as if he would spit venom if he could. He was probably angry for the two of them: his brother who was recovering at the healer's and himself.

Kolbjorn clambered out of the mead bench. He needed to respond—respectfully. Now that he did not need Father's approval, he did not mind making him wait. He walked towards his father, his shoes rustling against the floor reeds. Then he stood right before him, their eyes locking.

The jarl was frowning, struggling to hide his anger. Kolbjorn noted with a strange satisfaction that now it was Bjorn who was waiting to see if his bastard would accept him as a father.

But Kolbjorn would. Of course he would. Doing otherwise would be the greatest insult to Jarl Bjorn, especially in front of the king.

"Father," he said. "This is everything I have ever wanted."

Kolbjorn's voice came out not as stiff as it would have before, but smooth, a diplomat's peace offering. The jarl's face relaxed. He got up and stood in front of Kolbjorn, put his hands on his son's shoulders and squeezed them tightly.

"You are not just Kolbjorn anymore. You are Kolbjorn Bjornsson!" he roared the last word, and the hall erupted in table hammering, roars and wolf's howls.

And then he added softly, just for Kolbjorn to hear, "Kolbjorn Bjornsson. The next leader of the pack. My heir."

Kolbjorn was still trying to get his head around everything that had happened as they began the winter deer hunt three days later.

It was a warm day, and sometimes bears would come out of their winter dens. As one did this day.

The beast was huge, and he stopped fifty feet or so away from them, sniffing the air, without any sign of aggression.

"The gods are smiling!" the king said to Jarl Bjorn. "I think a bear stew tonight and a bear fur cloak would do just fine. If you kill him, Bjorn, I will help you become a king by next Jul."

Kolbjorn glanced, worried, at the drunken smile that spread on his father's face.

"I think I would like that bear stew as well, Eirik. And being a king next year. Kolbjorn, Son, give me that spear."

Kolbjorn did not move a finger.

"Father, is this wise? Let the beast go."

"What? Kolbjorn, where did you lose your balls?"

"You are drunk."

"So? My hand is just as steady. Give me the spear."

Kolbjorn clenched his jaw. Fear for his father chilled his skin like a winter draft. He had to keep his father from being injured.

"Better I kill him for you."

Bjorn's face lost all amusement. "No."

"Looks like your new son thinks you are too old to handle a bear," Eirik said.

Bjorn snorted and took out his long hunting knife.

"Then I'll kill him with my own hands."

Before Kolbjorn could make a move to stop him, Bjorn growled, and with a roar, he darted towards the bear.

It ran at first, but it was slow from the snow and sleepy and weak from the long sleep and lack of food for weeks, and Bjorn reached it, sinking his knife right in between the shoulder blades. Kolbjorn was already on his way towards his father, his heart racing.

The bear, now enraged and fully awake, turned to Bjorn, roaring, biting, jaws flashing, claws slicing. The jarl was surprisingly quick for the amount of mead he had consumed during Jul. His knife slashed and sank.

But not fast enough.

Kolbjorn was already there when his father fell clutching at his side, a scarlet bloom spreading on the snow around him.

The bear rose, its pained, furious roar hurting Kolbjorn's ears. It was about to jump on Bjorn for the final deadly attack when Kolbjorn threw the spear. It pierced the mighty animal right in the chest, kicking it back a little, and its roar trailed off. It sank into the snow right at the jarl's feet.

When they brought Jarl Bjorn home, Kolbjorn, remembering Rachel's advice, wanted to tell the healers to wash and boil the linen before applying it to his father's wound. But it was too late; they'd already used the dirty rags.

After that, the jarl got rot-wound. Kolbjorn wished then that there was a necklace or a treasure or anything else that he could have stolen, fought for—died for, if necessary—that would make his father healthy again. He understood Rachel then like never before.

His father fought against the rot-wound, but it won.

In two weeks, he was dying. At his death bed stood Alfarr and Ebbe and Kolbjorn. Out of the three of them, he locked his eyes with Kolbjorn, and said, right in front of everyone, "There is no father more proud of his son. Be the best jarl this land can have."

Kolbjorn's eyes burned. He wished Rachel was by his side. She had been right all along. When he'd stopped caring what his father thought and started living by his own rules, he'd gotten everything he had wanted—except that he had no father now.

Nor the woman he loved more than life itself.

BUSKELAND, Norway, June 875 AD

KOLBJORN THREW the sack with oats onto the longship, the breeze cooling his bare chest pleasantly. It was not a jarl's job, but he hated the idea of putting himself above his warrior brothers, who had always protected his back in the raids and always would. Kolbjorn had learned that besides Ulf, Garpr and Haki, the rest of the warriors from the village had remained loyal to him, refusing to hunt him down with his brothers.

His muscles sang from the physical exercise, and he was looking forward to the satisfying burn he'd feel in his shoulders after rowing for a long time. A breeze brought the scent of the sea from beyond the curve of the fjord, enticing him.

Kolbjorn hoped the adventure would be a pleasant distraction that would stop him thinking about Rachel every moment of his life.

They were setting sail later today, after all the ships were loaded with necessary cargo and they had made a sacrifice to the gods for a successful journey.

This would be his first raid as jarl.

Jarl Kolbjorn Bjornsson.

But now he wanted other things.

What he wanted most was Rachel. Kolbjorn, a bastard just a few moons ago, was the new jarl. But it did not matter. Not one bit.

Because now he had no father. And he had no Rachel.

The world around Kolbjorn faded as he remembered standing on this pier a few moons earlier, his heart bleeding...

The burning ship bearing Jarl Bjorn's body sailed slowly down the fjord between the mountains. The world would never be the same. He wished Rachel was standing next to him. He wanted to feel her soft hand in his, to feel her reassurance and understanding. Her love.

"I love you," she had said.

He was still watching the ship when snow started falling quietly, the breeze whispering, and he thought that in between the snowflakes brushing his ears, he felt the cold, wet kisses of the Valkyries who had come to take his father to Valhalla, and they promised Kolbjorn he'd meet his father there one day.

His brothers had left the jarldom after the burial, even though Kolbjorn had promised them places on the raiding ships. Alfarr was a cripple now and could not fight well.

Ebbe was a coward who had always been at the back of the battle.

Kolbjorn returned to the here and now with a jolt, then threw another sack of oats grown by his people at his village. His home.

Thanks to the alliance with King Eirik, the Swedes were not a threat anymore, and Kolbjorn was building a peaceful and prosperous new home. And he missed Rachel so much that his very bones hurt. If he could trade the jarldom, his name, all his silver and gold, for just one night with her, he would.

He had gone often to the sacred grove, praying, making sacrifices, demanding that the Norns give Rachel back to him. Once or twice he thought he saw a movement behind the trees, her cloak, a swish of auburn hair, but when he looked, she was not there.

And he bled inside, the pain so strong, as if a hammer pounded at his bones making them crack and crumble like rocks.

He straightened up after throwing the last sack onto the ship, the warm early summer breeze tickling his sweat-slicked skin. Strangely, the breeze brought the scent of sweet apples that was forever linked to her, and his chest ached as if pierced by a blade. He needed to forget her. But he knew that even on his death bed, she'd be the only one in his thoughts.

He turned to walk to the village and saw an auburn-haired figure in a woolen cloak standing on the pier.

His heart stopped, his very bone marrow buzzing.

He wiped his eyes, then squinted to be sure he was not dreaming.

She smiled.

Rachel.

CHAPTER EIGHTEEN

RACHEL THOUGHT her heart would stop at the sight of him. Her pulse tapped in her temples, her stomach flipping, her mouth dry.

Kolbjorn looked even more gorgeous than she remembered. The muscles of his chest and shoulders rolled like waves, and his skin glistened with sweat as he threw the sacks into the ship, his ripped stomach tensing and relaxing. Rachel could almost smell his masculine scent, almost taste the salt of his skin, and her knees grew weak.

But then he saw her, their eyes connecting, and the world stopped spinning. He was breathing heavily. Undoubtedly from the exercise, not from seeing her.

She could sense that there was something different about him. It was as if he had grown taller, his shoulders straight, his head high.

And he was going away.

She shivered despite the sun's heat.

"Are you going somewhere?" she said.

How dumb. Out of all things she could say, she said that?

He watched her with an expression of disbelief, as if he thought exactly the same. She blushed.

"Yes," he said. "I am."

Rachel's hands shook. She'd hoped they'd connect again like before once they saw each other, as if nothing existed but them.

But something was wrong.

She walked towards him, her thick-soled winter boots thumping softly against the wood of the pier.

He watched her with a frown, his chest rising and falling, but did not move. No sign of joy, no movement towards her.

Had he forgotten her? Had he met someone else?

The thought stabbed her like a blade to the stomach, and she almost doubled up.

"Where are you going?" she asked, stopping in front of him. She slid the heavy backpack she was carrying from her shoulder. It held all the treasure she had promised, and more.

His warmth radiated and tickled her skin. Her lips itched to kiss him, her hands almost lifting to touch his beard, to feel his strong body under her fingertips. Her body swung slightly towards him, as if drawn by an invisible magnet, anxious to feel his arms pulling her into his warm embrace.

But he stood still as a mountain, piercing her with his hazel eyes.

"On a raid. To Pictland."

"Oh. Scotland. For how long?"

"Until the ships are full with treasure."

"Won't your wife miss you?" The word "wife" broke in half like a dry twig.

He blinked. "No."

Rachel nodded. "Do you have a wife?"

"No."

She let out a laugh, relief slipping through the nervous smile on her face.

"How long have I been gone?"

"Half a year," he said, then added so softly, almost in a whisper, "Are you really here?"

Tension evaporated from Rachel's forehead. "Yes," she said. "I really am."

She reached out and took his left hand in both of hers. She was afraid he'd jerk it away or reject her in some other way. But once her palms reached his, he squeezed her fingers and looked down. Then he slowly drew her hands towards his face and studied them carefully, and her skin burned.

His palm was warm and dry, his skin calloused and rough, and pleasant heat spread through her.

Then he pressed them against his lips, his wet touch sending tingles through her, his eyes closing, the skin around them wrinkling. He held her hands like this for a long while, and Rachel's worry started melting away, her stomach unclenching, her lungs expanding.

He was not indifferent. A tear rolled down her cheek.

"It's really you," he whispered against her fingers, warming them with his breath. "I can feel your hand. It's as soft as I remember. I thought I'd never see you again."

Rachel could not stand a second more of not being in his arms. She stepped towards him, and he opened himself to her. And once she was in his arms, the world stood still again.

Her hands closed behind his back. His smell enveloped her: the sea, the sun, his fresh sweat. She inhaled it as if it were oxygen she needed to stay alive. She heard his heartbeat under her ear, beating as fast as her own.

"Why are you here?" She felt Kolbjorn's words warm against her ear, the very sound of his voice making her knees weak.

"I'm back," she said, still not letting him go. But he leaned back and studied her.

"Back?"

She swallowed. This was the hard part. To tell him that she had no intention of returning to her own time. To open her heart to him, to put it at his mercy.

"Yeah. For good. If you'll have me," she added.

Kolbjorn's eyes widened. "What of your mother?"

Rachel smiled broadly. "She's well, thanks to you. Thanks to the necklace."

Kolbjorn's shoulders relaxed. "That is good news. How did you come back?"

"Well. I did not have the golden spindle anymore. So I had to look for the Norn. It was not easy, mind you. In Chicago, those who follow pagan culture celebrate the Jul festival, and that was where I found her. She said she enjoyed our story the most and thought that I'd come find her earlier. You were right —she knew everything. And she said I should get my things and she'd send me back, but for the last time. I wouldn't be able to return to my time anymore."

Kolbjorn eyes widened. "You won't?"

"No, I'm stuck here. I came here to redeem myself, and I brought this wergild, I suppose." She lifted the backpack. "There's wine and hot dogs, painkillers and medicine that kills infections—rot-wounds. And there are more gemstones— synthetic ones, like the sapphires. Will you accept this as wergild for my theft?"

"No."

Rachel's heart sank. "Why not? I can also assist the jewelry master until my debt is paid."

He shook his head. "This is not good enough, Rachel."

"What else can I do?"

"I'll accept you here, allow you to work with the jewelry

master and accept your wergild"—he nodded towards the backpack—"under one condition."

"What?"

"That you'll be my wife."

Rachel opened her mouth but not a word came out. Had she heard him right? Had he just proposed? Her mouth went dry.

She slapped his chest slightly with her hand and smiled. "So you do have a trickster inside of you."

He only cocked his head. "What do you say? Do you want to be a jarl's wife?"

"A *jarl's* wife? Are you a jarl now?"

"I am."

"That means he accepted you?"

He nodded.

"He would be a fool if he hadn't. Wait. If you are a jarl, where is your father?"

"He died this winter."

Her heart squeezed for him. He had now lost both of his parents. Rachel pressed her face against his chest. "I am so sorry, Kolbjorn!"

She looked up and studied his face, and, as usual, he looked stoically at her.

"Will you not need an honorable wife as a jarl?"

"I no longer care what anyone thinks. You were right. I needed to live by my own rules. And as soon as I started, I got everything I had ever wanted. Except the thing I wanted most. You."

Rachel smiled softly, feeling their souls connect on some level she could not grasp.

"You will be a good partner. You brought treasures and medicine, and you are ready to redeem yourself. Which you will do, don't get me wrong. You must return what you stole in some way or another. The love and dedication that you showed to your mother, that you showed to me, by coming back here—with the wergild—tells me that you will be the best partner any man could hope for. What do you say?"

There was one thing she had to know before she'd commit to him.

"I said something before I left. Do you remember?"

"I remember."

He traced his fingers down her cheek gently, the caress sending waves of sweet anticipation through her skin. She leaned into his touch slightly.

"What did I say?"

"That you loved me." His thumb slid down to her mouth and he traced her lip gently, igniting her skin.

"So before I give my answer to you," she said, seeing his pupils dilate while he watched her lip move under his thumb. "I need to know. Do you love me?"

He brought his gaze back to hers, their eyes locking as they had the first time they met. His hands went to his neck, and he removed something from under his tunic. It was the necklace that Rachel's mother made for her, that she had left with Jarl Bjorn. She touched it with her fingers and noticed it held the warmth of his body. Tears welled in her eyes. He'd kept it with him, next to his heart, all along.

"I do. With every drop of my blood, with every part of my soul, with every corner of my heart. I love you, my time traveler."

His words melted the last bits of tension within Rachel like fire melted snow, and she allowed herself the broadest, happiest smile of her life.

"Then I will marry you, my Viking."

She reached up for him and finally claimed the lips she had been craving to kiss for so long. He took her mouth hungrily, as if he feared that the next second she'd be gone, and he needed to take everything he could get. He lifted her with his hands, her legs wrapping around his thighs, her sex pressed against his rock-hard erection, sending waves of pleasure through her as he began walking.

"I must have you," he growled against her mouth. "Life robbed me of you, and I must replenish all the time I have lost."

Rachel looked down as he stepped over the hull of the longship. "What? Right here?"

He walked to the furthest corner of the ship, where the piles of sacks and barrels stood. The bottom shifted, making Rachel's head spin even more and adding to the burning through her whole body. He sank to his knees together with her right behind a little hill of goods.

"Yes. Here. Anywhere."

They sank to the bottom, shielded now from any prying eyes from the village, and as Kolbjorn's lips found Rachel's again, she melted in his strong arms and they breathed and moved as one. Finally, Rachel felt complete, and as she gazed into Kolbjorn's warm eyes, she knew he felt it, too.

EPILOGUE

BUSKELAND, NORWAY, FIVE YEARS LATER

KOLBJORN LOOKED over his mead hall, which swarmed with people. Eruptions of laughter, drunken stories, the friendly and unfriendly banter of men who had drunk too much rang around it. The giant, dim room was warm and smelled like a feast: fermented honey, roasted meat, cooked vegetables.

He, as always, had a clear head—clear of alcohol, anyway.

But it was pleasantly full with thoughts of his family, who were near him. His wife sat by his great chair, the auburn-haired witch from the future who had brought him more happiness than he could ever grasp, ever take in. Her hand hung from the chair arm as did his, and they touched ever so slightly, barely noticeable to anyone, the connection of their skin slight but the invisible connection of their souls unbreakable.

His two-year-old son, Bjorn, slept in their bedchamber, lulled by the hum of the feast. He had Kolbjorn's brown hair, but Kolbjorn did not think of his son as a cur. He did not think like that about himself anymore, either.

Kolbjorn was the son of the jarl and always had been, whether he had the official name or not. It was in his blood.

And it was in his son's and the second child that Rachel was carrying.

King Eirik sat on Kolbjorn's other side with a pretty servant girl on his lap, his eyes glossy. He had just renewed the alliance that he had taken away after Jarl Bjorn died. Rubies glistened on the golden Mjölnir pendant around his neck, the most masterful jewelry Kolbjorn had ever seen.

When the king's eyes had fallen on the pendant, he had not moved for a moment. "Did Thor himself make it?"

"No. My wife," Kolbjorn had said, pride puffing his chest.

Rachel had hidden a smile with a slight bow of her head, the sign of modesty and respect. Rachel had crafted the pendant specially for the king himself, as a gift and to ensure his alliance with Kolbjorn.

A movement caught his eyes, and he saw three people approaching through the mead benches—a woman, a man, and a child. Kolbjorn's guards shifted, as well as every warrior in the hall, ready to protect their jarl, his wife, and King Eirik at any sign of a wrong move, but Kolbjorn made a slight gesture with his hand, and the men relaxed a little, still wary.

The man coming towards Kolbjorn looked familiar. In the weathered face, he recognized Ebbe.

Kolbjorn exchanged a glance with Rachel. She was clearly as surprised as he was.

"Ebbe Bjornsson," Kolbjorn said. "What brings you here?"

Ebbe bowed slightly. "This is my wife, Liv, and my daughter, Aslaug."

Kolbjorn nodded in acknowledgment. Seeing his half-brother brought a feeling of sadness at the memory of their father, who was not among them anymore, and the memory of his brothers' betrayal.

"What did you come for, Ebbe? We did not part as the best of friends."

"No. We did not. And I regret it."

Kolbjorn felt his eyebrows rise in surprise. "*You* regret it?"

"I do. I have always been drawn into Alfarr's plans, always a follower. But ever since I married and started my own family, I realized that I no longer want to follow another man's lead, especially not a man like Alfarr. I must decide how to raise my daughter, and I do not want her to become like Alfarr. Like me."

Rachel leaned towards Kolbjorn and whispered with a smile, "I am sure it's Liv's doing. She must be a good woman."

"Are you coming to make peace?" Kolbjorn asked, still not quite believing that his brother would do that.

"I am," he said with a bow. "And I have come to beg your protection. Alfarr has angered the neighboring chieftain. His warriors killed Alfarr, and now they are coming for us, to destroy our farm."

Kolbjorn felt a small stab of pain at the news of Alfarr's death, even though he was not surprised, and part of him felt that his brother likely deserved what he'd gotten.

"We are just farmers," Ebbe continued. "Not warriors. I cannot protect my family on my own. I am asking for your help."

Kolbjorn glanced at the king, who eyed the whole conversation with great interest. Undoubtedly, he realized who Ebbe was. Kolbjorn looked at Rachel, and she gave him a small nod. They were both thinking the same. Family was family. Kolbjorn would not allow this little girl to grow up without a mother and a father. He did not hold a grudge against Ebbe, did not feel the need for revenge against him, like many others would. His father had recognized Kolbjorn and valued him more than his legitimate sons.

Kolbjorn had won a long time ago.

"I will help you," he said, and gratitude flooded Ebbe's and Liv's faces. "I will send twenty warriors. That should be enough?"

"Yes. Yes. Thank you, brother."

It was the first time that Ebbe had called Kolbjorn that, and a smile touched his lips as the forgotten desire to have a brother returned. "Join the feast. Eat. Drink. Stay."

Ebbe's eyes burned. "You are not a mongrel, Kolbjorn, and never have been, no matter what Alfarr said." Ebbe's voice was low, but Kolbjorn heard him, and his eyes prickled. "You are the wolf," his brother finished, bowing again before finding a seat with his wife and daughter.

When Kolbjorn looked at Rachel, she gave him a small signal—the special way she rubbed her cheek—that they had agreed on, to find a place for just the two of them. He wanted to go to the bedchamber with her, but she led him out of the mead hall. "I want some fresh air."

They excused themselves before the king and went outside. The warm summer evening was quiet. It smelled like the sea and lilacs.

Without pause, Rachel led Kolbjorn up the hill towards the sacred grove, and a chill ran across his skin.

"Where are you going? You are not going back to your time, are you?"

She laughed, and the sound of it always made something melt inside him.

"No, silly. Like I told you countless times, I'm not going anywhere. You are stuck with me forever."

"Thank the gods," he said with a relieved sigh.

"It's just quiet in the grove because people are afraid of

going near it after they saw me disappear. And I want a peaceful moment alone with you. Bjorn is sleeping, and I don't want to listen to people getting drunk on the other side of that thin wall while we are doing what I have in mind."

He liked where this was going. "And what is that?"

They passed by Kolbjorn's old house, the place where they had first seen each other. The moment that had changed their lives.

She did not say anything, just looked at him and wiggled her eyebrows. It always made him laugh.

"I am pregnant, I am horny, and I want you."

"Happy to oblige, wife."

When they arrived at the clearing, Kolbjorn laid his fur cloak on the ground. His heart sung as he planted a kiss on her lips, the first of many in what he hoped would be a long night.

"You know what I just realized?" Rachel asked as he began kissing her graceful neck, inhaling the sweet scent of apples that always made him feel more alive.

"What?" he murmured against her skin.

"The Necklace of Northern Lights... It brought us together. Through time. It saved my mother. It connected us. Without it, we would not be here. It's the jewel of time."

Kolbjorn leaned back slightly to look at her, to see her translucent skin, silvery in the darkness, the dark ruby undertone of her auburn hair, the pearls of her teeth.

"No," he said. "It's not the necklace. It's you."

Rachel smiled a shy little smile.

He cupped her jaw. "You are my jewel of time."

Thank you for reading VIKING'S LOVE. I hope you loved Cathy and Andor's story. Find out what happens next when the

Norns send Mia to meet her soulmate Hakon the Beast in VIKING'S CAPTIVE.

ENEMIES BECOME lovers when a powerful Viking jarl takes a beautiful time traveler captive. Have the fates sent him a good omen or a curse?

READ VIKING'S CAPTIVE now >

"WOW! I absolutely loved this story!"

SIGN-UP FOR MARIAH STONE'S Newsletter:

http://mariahstone.com/signup

FANCY A HIGHLANDER?

And other mysterious matchmakers are sending people to the past too, also to the Highlands. If you haven't read Craig and Amy's story yet, be sure to pick up HIGHLANDER'S CAPTIVE.

In her arms he finds strength. In his arms she finds hope. Can their love outlast the ages?

ONE-CLICK HIGHLANDER'S CAPTIVE now >

⭐⭐⭐⭐⭐ *"One of the MOST ROMANTIC AND HEART WRENCHING TALES I've read in a long while! Absolutely loved it!"*

Or stay in the Viking Age and read an excerpt from VIKING'S CAPTIVE.

New York City, 2018

Donna Cox had to win the case, or four clients would not be able to buy bread next month. They waited for the hearing in a court waiting room. Marta and Helena sat to her right, ripe like watermelons. To Donna's left, Teresa and Gloria, both single mothers, whispered in Spanish while rocking two strollers that looked like their best days were long behind.

All four women had been cleaners in a big company, Cinderellas Inc. Their supervisor had fired them as soon as he'd found out they were pregnant. Donna was glad they were brave enough to sue. Most women in their situation did not dare.

Donna's phone rang, and the word "Mom" lit up the screen. Mother was Donna's partner in their two-woman law firm in Brooklyn. Donna held up her index finger to her clients to signal that she'd be right back and went out into the hall.

"Mom? I can't talk. I'm about to go in for the hearing."

"That's why I'm calling. There's been a change, and I'll need you to keep your cool."

"A change?"

"Yes. I found out a minute ago. Ferguson and Partners replaced Virginia with—darn it—with Daniel Gleason."

Heat spread over Donna's cheeks. Daniel Gleason represented everything she passionately despised in the world and the reason she specialized in discrimination lawsuits.

New York swarmed with Daniel Gleasons, and they enjoyed way too much power over women. They ran law firms, hedge funds, and insurance companies. Sometimes, they taught at schools, drove cabs, and mixed cocktails. And one of them had broken Donna's heart.

Daniel looked like a Norse god in a suit. A typical alpha male, he thought only pretty women should be secretaries and that all female CEOs and politicians were lesbians. Three years ago, he had insisted that Donna should stop working, find a rich husband, and give birth to five sons. Back then she had secretly hoped he wanted to be that husband. Despite herself, she had considered following his suggestion because she was in love.

Thank heavens she hadn't. Not that he'd ever proposed. In retrospect, she was glad he'd stopped sleeping with her one day. He'd taught her a lesson.

The lesson she'd thought was part of her DNA, something her single mother had fed her every day with breakfast. To never—*ever*—fall in love with a mouthwatering hunk with a big ego and a sexy smile.

That was why she only dated geeks—often writers or web designers. Guys who respected women. So what if the sex was as stale as day-old champagne. They were smart and funny. They begged her for another date, not the other way around.

"Donna? Are you there?"

Donna blinked, her hand shook. "Yes, Mom."

"Honey. Listen to me. This is the most important lawsuit of

your career. Our career. This could be huge for our firm. Put aside your anger. Are you sure you can manage?"

Donna let out a long breath. It didn't help. "I bet this is precisely why they put him on the case."

Mom sighed. "They know the type of men we fight against. Still. You can do it."

"All right. I'm going back in."

"Good luck."

Donna hung up and shook her hands to relieve the pressure. When she went back into the waiting room, an older woman was in her seat. She looked like a universal grandma in small, round spectacles. She knit a wide scarf with a pattern of interwoven tree branches—it reminded Donna of Celtic or Viking art. A golden spindle lay on her lap. Donna did not have time to think about how peculiar she was, because right next to the woman, on Marta's seat, was Daniel.

Donna froze as if she'd hit a glass wall. She had not seen him for three years, and he looked even yummier—and more arrogant—than before. Tall, broad-shouldered, and perfectly built, he sat with his long legs stretched out and ankles crossed. He watched her with a patronizing smirk as if she was a cute little kitten about to fight a bull.

Donna's cheeks flushed from the embarrassment of the unresolved past, and hate burned her like acid. He was using her past feelings against her by being here.

She frowned. Something was wrong in this picture.

Her eight-month pregnant client was standing, rubbing her lower back, leaning against the wall and grimacing in pain, while this son of a butterfly sat on her chair as if he were waiting for a massage in a Turkish sauna.

No. This had not just happened! Fury lit her blood on fire. Donna marched towards them, her heels clacking murder against the marble floor of the courthouse.

"What do you think you are doing, Daniel? You self-centered orangutan! Did you take a pregnant woman's seat? Did you tell her to go back to Mexico? Do you realize we can sue you personally for this? We have witnesses." She pointed at the old lady.

Daniel's face lost all color, and the smirk dropped down his face like a wet towel.

He jumped to his feet. "Donna— No, I'd never— I didn't—"

This was new. She had never seen him stutter like this. Maybe she should throw accusations at him more often.

Marta glanced sheepishly at her. "Donna, as much as I enjoy the show, Mr. Gleason did not steal my seat. My lower back is killing me. I needed to walk."

Mortification struck Donna like a wet snowball. Daniel crossed his arms over his chest, the arrogant smirk lighting up his face again.

"Who will sue now, Donna? But, I feel generous. I'm willing to forget your insults if I can buy you a drink after I win today. Would be great to catch up."

Donna took a deep breath. She realized Daniel had gotten what he'd come for. He shook her off balance, made her emotional, and showed her who was in control.

No, she wouldn't give him the satisfaction. She was a great lawyer. A Harvard graduate. She needed to show him his place. If only she could find the confidence. Everyone was looking at Donna—even the old lady, a sly little smile spreading her lips.

"You know what, Daniel. I will never let you win. You can shove your drink up your nose."

She knew she sounded ridiculous, but anger and embarrassment choked her throat. Why could she not do trash talk?

Donna turned her back to Daniel and, pretending to look through the lawsuit documents, went out of the waiting room into the hall like a high school girl. Thankfully, the hallway was empty, so she could take a breath for a moment.

"Excuse me—Donna, is it?"

Donna turned around, her cheeks still on fire. The old lady with the knitting stood behind her.

"Yes?" Donna took a step towards her.

The woman studied her with the curiosity of a scientist. She had an accent Donna couldn't place. "I could not help but overhear. It seems you have an issue with strong men."

Donna frowned. "I do not have an issue with strong men!"

"Oh, you do, dear. I need you somewhere. No, wrong. There is a man who needs you."

"Needs me? As a lawyer? I mostly represent women against men, so—"

The lady smiled. "Exactly. Could you hold this for me please?"

She held out the spindle, which Donna now noticed was carved tree branches, snakes, and leaves, knotted together in an unending pattern. Donna wondered distantly, who would use a spindle nowadays? Her palm closed around it.

The metal burned her fingertips like a hot cup of tea after a cold day, smooth and sharp. The waiting room disappeared. It was as if something sucked Donna's blood out of her body, a thousand of axes cut her flesh, and a furnace melted her bones. She screamed in pain but only heard the chanting of a man, and she spun and spun like the golden spindle.

And then there was nothing...

Keep reading **VIKING'S CAPTIVE.**

Also by Mariah Stone

MARIAH'S TIME TRAVEL ROMANCE SERIES

- CALLED BY A HIGHLANDER
- CALLED BY A VIKING
- CALLED BY A PIRATE
- FATED

MARIAH'S REGENCY ROMANCE SERIES

- DUKES AND SECRETS

VIEW ALL OF MARIAH'S BOOKS IN READING ORDER

Scan the QR code for the complete list of Mariah's ebooks, paperbacks, and audiobooks in reading order.

GET A FREE MARIAH STONE BOOK!

Join Mariah's mailing list to be the first to know of new releases, free books, special prices, and other author giveaways.

freehistoricalromancebooks.com

ENJOY THE BOOK? YOU CAN MAKE A DIFFERENCE!

Please, leave your honest review for the book.

As much as I'd love to, I don't have financial capacity like New York publishers to run ads in the newspaper or put posters in subway.

But I have something much, much more powerful!

Committed and loyal readers.

If you enjoyed the book, I'd be so grateful if you could spend five minutes leaving a review on the book's **sales page.**

Thank you very much!

ACKNOWLEDGMENTS

There are several people who have helped this book to see the light of day. THANK YOU:

Laura Barth, my editor, who is the only person besides my husband with whom I keep messaging daily.

My husband, my rock, who keeps encouraging me, supporting me, and holding my hand.

My parents who did everything to help me make my dreams come true.

My writer friends, you know who you are.

About Mariah Stone

Mariah Stone is a bestselling author of time travel romance novels, including her popular Called by a Highlander series and her hot Viking, Pirate, and Regency novels. With nearly one million books sold, Mariah writes about strong modern-day women falling in love with their soulmates across time. Her books are available worldwide in multiple languages in e-book, print, and audio.

Subscribe to Mariah's newsletter for a free time travel book today at mariahstone.com/signup!

facebook.com/mariahstoneauthor

instagram.com/mariahstoneauthor

bookbub.com/authors/mariah-stone

pinterest.com/mariahstoneauthor

amazon.com/Mariah-Stone/e/B07JVW28PJ

www.ingramcontent.com/pod-product-compliance
Lightning Source LLC
LaVergne TN
LVHW040009250525
812154LV00009B/329